SPOTLIGHT

BOOK #3 IN THE GUARDIAN SERIES

PIPER DAVENPORT

Cathy—
Much love!
Piper Davenport

Spotlight is a work of fiction. Names, characters, places, and incidents are the products of the author's imagination and are used fictitiously. Any resemblance to actual events, locales, or persons, living or dead, is entirely coincidental.

Cover Art
Jackson Jackson

TRIXIE PUBLISHING

2019 Piper Davenport
Copyright © 2019 by Trixie Publishing, Inc.
All rights reserved.

ISBN-13: 9781090124104

Published in the United States

SPOTLIGHT

BOOK #3 IN THE GUARDIAN SERIES

Liz Kelly:
Thanks again. Your insight is always so spot on!

Jack:
Thanks for all laughs and inspiration for the sexy bits!

Brandy, Gail & Kathren:
Ladies, I couldn't do this without you! Thanks for all
your read throughs!

ONE

Harmony

"DIDI, THIS ISN'T a good idea," I warned. My sister, Melody, was currently sitting in a makeup chair, her ever-faithful makeup slave, Billy, practicing his prosthetics to make her look like a completely different person.

"It's all good, NiNi," she argued while trying not to move her mouth.

"Someone is *stalking* you!" I snapped. "You need to stay here...where it's safe."

"*Girl*, she won't look anything like Melody

Morgan, international pop and movie star," Billy crooned, his swishiness on overdrive. "She's gonna look like my high school girlfriend."

"You had a high school girlfriend?" I challenged.

"Yep. And a boyfriend." He thrust out his hip and waved his hand. "Decided I liked the boy better."

"That's right, baby," Graham, his boyfriend, retorted from his seat in the corner.

"Dork." I giggled. I loved Billy in all his dramatic glory. He'd been "with" us for ten years and he was one of my favorite people on the planet.

My phone buzzed in my pocket and I pulled it out to see: *Lyric Calling.* "Hey LiLi."

"Hi, honey, did you talk some sense into DiDi?"

Lyric was our eldest sister, and most days I felt like it was her and me against the world... or at the very least, her and me trying to keep Melody from making more stupid decisions.

"No." I sighed. "Billy's making her look different, but I don't know if that will help."

"Put her on speaker," Melody demanded, and I did. "LiLi, we are in a new city, I want to explore."

"Might I point out, you've been here before.

For three months of shooting and I recall you exploring then, too."

"But that was, like, two years ago. I want to see what's new."

"I get that, honey," Lyric said in her 'patient' voice, "but you're going out with a man you've only met twice."

"He's in the movie with me, sissy," she countered. "I'm going to see him every day for the next four months."

Melody was in the blockbuster sequel to the blockbuster film adapted from a local author's romance novels, so we were in Portland to film. She also had two singles she'd wrote for each of the movies, which had gone platinum three times over, so she was famous on every level.

Lyric had a real job as an attorney, so she stayed behind in Savannah, however, I was Melody's assistant, so I was with her…as always.

"*Sweetness*, he is a new character and has *not* been vetted," Lyric ground out.

Melody and I rolled our eyes, almost in sync. Whenever Lyric called one of us "sweetness," we knew she was beyond irritated.

Lyric was two years older than me and six years older than Melody. She'd been a second mother to us, especially considering our own mother had a tendency to sleep all day and drink all night. Our father died almost thirteen years ago, right around the time Melody "hit" big as a kid star. Mom's cirrhosis of the liver caught up to her two years ago and we'd buried another parent. Our lives were irrevocably rocked, in both good and bad ways.

Tonight fell into the bad category.

"I've made a few calls," Lyric continued. "So, would you please stay in? Just for tonight. I've got a new security person coming tomorrow."

Melody let out a loud, dramatic sigh. "Fine, I'll stay in," she said, as she shook her head.

"Thanks, DiDi. I'll talk to y'all tomorrow." Lyric hung up and I slid my phone back in my pocket.

"If you're insisting on being an idiot, I'm coming with you," I threatened.

"No, you're not."

"Mel—"

"No. It's all good. I'm taking Butchy, he'll watch out for me."

"Butchy's almost as famous as you are," I snapped. "If you take him, they'll know it's you."

"Hmm, you have a point." She waved Billy away and swiveled her chair to face me. "I'll take Arnold."

4

Julian 'Butch' Maren was head of our security team, but unfortunately he was gorgeous, and highly photogenic, so he tended to get as much coverage as Melody. At least he was really good at his job and could take down several men at one time, but it had become harder and harder for him to protect her, so he'd put a team together to take over.

"Ohmigod, Melody, don't *do* this."

A knock at the door interrupted my argument, and I let out a frustrated squeak.

"Get that, will you NiNi?" Melody directed. "I'm almost ready."

* * *

Jaxon

My phone buzzed just as I stepped out of the shower and I almost ignored it, but I was waiting for my partner to call me about a case we'd been looking into, so I swiped it off the counter and answered it. "Jaxon Quinn."

"Jax, hey, it's Mack."

Mack Reed was part of the Dogs of Fire Motorcycle Club—the same club two of my brothers belonged to—and he and I had formed a pretty strong brotherhood of our own. His wife, Darien, was a bestselling romance author who'd had her first two books turned into movies and had just started shooting the second.

"Hey, man. What's up?"

"Dare and I have a favor."

I frowned. If Mack was asking for a favor, this wasn't good. "What's going on?"

"Melody Morgan's bein' stalked."

Melody was the kid star, pop princess, generally entitled hot mess, starring in Darien's movies, and having met the woman, I wasn't a fan.

"And this is your problem because…?"

Mack let out a sigh. "Dare's worried."

I rubbed my forehead. "Enough to ask you to call me to see if I can use my FBI resources to figure it out," I deduced.

"Yeah."

"She didn't want to call me directly?"

"You know Darien enough to know she thinks I'll get more results."

I smiled. "Tell her next time she needs a favor to ask me directly. I like her better than you."

Mack chuckled. "I'll do that."

"Let me call Matt and see what we can do."

"Appreciate it, brother."

I hung up and called my older brother (I was third in the line of six brothers). Matt was my boss at the FBI and although he was a by-the-book man, he often gave me and my partners,

Brock and Dallas, a lot of leeway when it came to bringing cases in.

"Hey, Jax, give me a second," Matt said. I heard rustling and then total silence. "Hey, brother, how are you?"

"I'm good. Got a call from Mack."

"Yeah?"

"Got a situation."

"Of course you do," he deadpanned.

I filled him in on what I knew and Matt sighed. "You've got forty-eight hours to figure out if this is a real threat or if the local cops can deal with it."

"That works," I said. "I'll call you tomorrow."

"Bye," he said, and hung up.

I finished getting dressed, then called Mack again.

"Hey, man," he said.

"Put Darien on," I said.

I heard rustling, then Darien said, "Hi, Jax."

"Hey, babe. What do you know about this Melody thing?"

"Not much, honestly," she said. "All I know for sure is that Harmony's totally freaked."

"Who's Harmony?"

"Her sister…and assistant."

"There's another one?" I ground out.

Darien chuckled. "No, there isn't another Melody. There's a Harmony and she's amazing, Jax, seriously. Super cool, very sweet, and really scared for her sister."

I sighed. "Okay. You want to reach out and see if she can meet me today?"

"Yes," she said, sounding relieved. "Thanks, Jaxon. I really appreciate it."

"No problem, Dare. Just let me know where to meet her."

"I will. Talk to you soon."

She hung up and Jaxon headed to his kitchen to grab something to eat, quickly realizing he hadn't had time to stop at the store once he got back from Alabama. As he grabbed his car keys to head out, his phone buzzed.

Darien: *Harmony will meet you at the Sentinel in an hour if that works.*

I texted back, *Works for me. What room?*

Darien: *Ask for Flossie Williams at the Concierge.*

I rolled my eyes. Fuck me, these starlets were nuts. I texted Darien back and told her I'd be there, then decided to grab dinner on the way.

* * *

Harmony

Melody had left an hour ago and I'd spent that

8

time pacing my hotel room, wringing my hands. Darien's phone call had kept me from grabbing a cab and hunting down my little sister…then handcuffing her to her bed until she was called to the set.

That last part might have been a little aggressive, but by the time I got to that line of thought, I was beyond worried and a little pissed off.

My room phone rang and I rushed to answer it. "Hello?"

"Miss Flossie?"

"Hmm-mm."

"This is the concierge. There's a Jaxon Quinn here to see you, ma'am."

"Is he the FBI agent?" I whispered, then cleared my throat. I didn't know why I was whispering. I was alone in my room.

"Yes ma'am."

"Did you check his credentials?"

"Yes ma'am, and I photocopied them."

I relaxed. "Thank you so much. Do you have one of the conference rooms open?"

"Yes. I'll meet you in the lobby and show you both."

"Excellent. Thank you."

"My pleasure."

We hung up and I grabbed my phone, folder

full of evidence, and room key and headed downstairs. As my elevator car took me to the person I hoped would protect my sister, I tapped my foot with nervous energy. The bell dinged, the doors opened…and my heart stopped.

Ohmigod, ohmigod, ohmi*god*!

The evening concierge, Adam was his name (I think), stood with the best looking man I'd ever seen in my life. Ever. Like as in everdom. Dark hair, a little shaggy on top, piercing blue eyes and a jaw that could rival Superman's, he was tall and built, and looked like he commanded the world. He wore jeans, a black long-sleeved Henley, with a black leather jacket and black motorcycle boots. When the man caught my eye, I swallowed and told myself to breathe. Then I forced myself to smile.

* * *

Jaxon

The elevator doors opened and I was a little taken aback by the beautiful woman who looked like she'd just seen something rather weird. I hoped it wasn't me, because, damn, she was gorgeous. Long blonde hair, light blue eyes and a curvy-as-sin body. She wore dark jeans and tight T-shirt, and she carried a manila envelope and a phone.

"Miss Morgan," Adam said.

"Adam," she said, and stepped out of the elevator.

"This is Agent Quinn."

I reached out to shake her hand and her cheeks pinkened as she slid her hand into mine. "It's nice to meet you," I said.

She licked her lips. "You too. Thank you so much for seeing me."

"If you'll follow me, I'll show you where you can speak privately," Adam said.

I stepped aside so Harmony could precede me and we followed Adam down a hallway and into a large conference room.

"Thanks, Adam," Harmony said.

Having her walk in front of me may have been a bad idea…her back end could only be described as perfection and I couldn't stop looking at her. Her ass had a heart shape to it which made me want to see it out of her jeans.

I was relieved that, although she looked like she was related to Melody, she didn't look too much like her. When I got Harmony under me, I didn't want to be thinking about her batshit crazy sibling.

We walked into the large conference room and the concierge left us alone, so I waved to one of the chairs at the table and we sat down.

"I'm sure you have a lot on your plate, Agent

Quinn," Harmony said. "But I really appreciate you taking time to have a look at this."

I nodded. "Start from the beginning."

"It started when we were here for the first movie shoot…," she scrolled through her phone and then slid it toward me. "This was the first 'gift.' We honestly didn't think much of it back then. Melody thought black roses were cool and told our security, but insisted we didn't take it further."

I forced myself to stay professional and not roll my eyes.

"I didn't think they were cool," Harmony finished.

This was obviously the smart sister. "I know this is a lot to ask, but what I'd like to have is dates, times, photos—"

"All in here," she interrupted, and slid the envelope toward me. "Copies of all of my notes, corresponding photos, and who was around those days."

I couldn't help but be impressed. "You had someone take notes?"

"*I* took notes," she corrected, then sighed. "My sister may not be taking this seriously, but I have been her protector since we were really little and I knew something was off. DiDi isn't the best judge of character. She tends to trust people

12

she shouldn't."

I didn't respond as I opened the envelope and pulled the paperwork out. I was once again impressed. "This is excellent, Miss Morgan."

"Harmony, please," she said. "Miss Morgan sounds so…I don't know…school girlish."

I chuckled to cover the fact I was suddenly thinking of her in a short uniform skirt and knee-high socks, sans panties. "Harmony. This is better than many of my agents could come up with. It's impressive."

"Well, I do have a bachelor's degree in criminal justice," she said, almost like she was embarrassed by it. "Not that I'm using it, currently."

There it was. A life interrupted that seemed like a waste to me.

"Did you take this to the local police?" I asked, veering the conversation back to the subject at hand.

She nodded. "I did at home."

"Home?"

"Savannah," she said. "But the cop was so enamored by my sister, he was of no use. He also wasn't overly concerned."

She had no worries I'd become enamored with her sister, but I kept that opinion to myself. "Has anyone new been hangin' around? Or, has anyone on your team been actin' strange?"

Harmony shook her head. "No. Everything's been business as usual." She rubbed her forehead and sighed. "Honestly, it's my sister who's the biggest problem. I love her, but man, she makes my life difficult."

I smiled. "Yeah?"

She nodded. "She's never been told no."

"And you?"

"Oh, I'm told no all the time."

I chuckled. "That sounds like a crime."

Her face blushed the cutest shade of red and she glanced away.

"Let me do some digging," I continued. "We'll figure out who's doin' this."

She let out a sigh of relief. "Thank you so much."

"Give me your phone."

She unlocked it and handed it to me without question, and I liked that she trusted me. I added my contact information, then texted myself before handing it back. "You see or hear anything concerning, you call me."

"Is…this your office number?" she asked, looking at her phone.

"No. It's my cell. Day or night, you feel squirrely, you call me, okay?"

She let out a quiet snort. "I'm not going to call you at night."

"Why not?"

"Um. Because it would be wrong?"

I smiled. "You need me, you call me."

"Will you come and kill a spider?" she asked. "Sorry, that was dumb. I shouldn't have said that. Of course, you won't come and kill a spider. I'm on my own for spider murder. Not even Billy will help me with arachnicide. Butchy might, but I honestly haven't asked him."

I forced my dick to stay down at her earnest expression. "You scared of spiders, Harmony?"

"Terrified is more accurate," she said, immediately, then waved her hands. "Please ignore me. I feel very safe with you, and now I'm just saying things out loud that make no sense, and I'm seriously about to lose my mind. Lordy, why can't I stop talking?"

Jesus, she was cute. And I loved that she felt safe with me. I tried not to chuckle at her rambling, but the more she talked in her quiet southern accent, the more I wanted to fuck her so hard she screamed my name.

I smiled slowly, waiting to see if she'd say anything else. When she didn't, I said, "You need me to kill a spider, Harmony, you feel free to call me."

She blushed again, but didn't say anything.

"Do you need me to make copies of all of

this?" I asked, tapping the folder.

"No. This is for you."

"Okay. I'm gonna head out and see what I can find, okay? If you think of anything else, let me know."

"Okay. Thanks, Agent Quinn."

"Jaxon."

She licked her lips. "Jaxon."

I nodded, and she walked me out to the lobby where we parted ways, but I knew I was gonna find a shit ton of excuses to see her again, even if it wasn't about finding her sister's stalker. My phone buzzed just as I slid into my truck, and I saw my youngest brother, Aidan, was calling. "Hey, brother.

"You comin' tomorrow?"

"Yeah, man, I'll see you there."

We all tried to make a Sunday night dinner rule amongst us kids. Our parents still lived several hours away, and my mother kept trying to break up every new relationship forming, so she was on a short list with Carter and Aidan. I had no dog in this fight. Not yet, anyway. Although, Harmony was the first woman to come along in a long time who piqued my interest.

I was fucked.

Jaxon

T HE NEXT AFTERNOON, I walked into my youngest brother's home and stalled. Aidan's daughter, Cambry, made a mad dash for me, and I scooped her up before her head could do permanent damage to my nuts.

"Unca Jax!" Cambry squeaked, and I hugged her close.

"Hey, baby."

"Oooh, quick reflexes you got there, buddy," Kimberly retorted as she approached us. She kissed my cheek and held her hands out for Cambry, but my niece was having none of it. She huffed and buried her head in my neck.

"She's good here, Kim," I said.

Kimberly was married to Aidan and they had two kids now. Since Kim was loaded, they lived in an historic home on a shit ton of land where they kept horses. Not that Aidan didn't do his part…he was a vet and the go-to Olympics equestrian trainer, which meant they were both sitting pretty when it came to money.

Kim chuckled. "Charmer."

"Her or me?" I asked.

"Both."

"Guilty." I grinned, and jostled Cambry gently. "How's my girl?"

She patted my face and gave me a toothy grin. "Mama said I could have ice cream."

"She did?"

She bobbed her head up and down.

"After dinner," Kimberly clarified.

Cambry wrinkled her nose but only so I could see and I forced myself not to laugh. At five years old, she was sassy as hell and I loved her for it.

"Where's Aidan?" I asked.

"At the grill. Ace is with him," Kim said. "Can I get you a beer?"

"Yeah, babe, that'd be great," I said, and followed her through the kitchen.

Kim held her arms out to her daughter. "Cambry, let's get you washed up."

I handed my niece off to Kim and headed out to the back patio. My brothers were part of the Dogs of Fire Motorcycle Club, and although I called them Carter and Aidan, their MC brothers called them Ace and Knight.

"Uncle Jax!" Liam, Carter's middle kid, called and made a run for me.

"Hey, bud," I said, hugging him quickly. "You helpin' Uncle Aidan man the grill?"

"Yeah. He even let me turn the ribs."

"Awesome."

"You get lost?" Carter asked, giving me a quick hug.

I chuckled. "Traffic."

"Of the female variety?"

"In a manner of speaking." The truth was, I'd been working on Harmony's case most of the day, without much luck. I'd also been trying to wrap my mind around the fact I was bummed out Harmony hadn't called or texted. It's not like I had expected her to, but I was still disappointed. "Where's Cass?" I asked.

"Puttin' Tillie down."

Carter and Cassidy had three kids. Maverick,

Liam, and Tillie. They had their hands full, but I was glad Carter was finally happy. He'd spent a hellava lot of years being separated from the only woman he loved and it took a hellava lot of work to get back to her.

"Hey, Jax," Cassidy said as she walked out to join us.

"Hey, babe," I said, and hugged her. "How's Tillie?"

"Feisty," she breathed out. "She did *not* want to miss out on the fun."

"I get it." I chuckled. "Where's Mav?"

"He's hanging with Lily tonight at Hawk and Payton's."

"Yeah? The marriage contract's been signed?"

Maverick and Lily had been in love with each other since they were little and it would appear it wasn't stopping anytime soon.

Cassidy grinned. "Pretty much. Maverick's got his proposal all planned out and everything."

"No shit?"

"No shit. I have a feeling he'll do it the second she graduates."

"And what does Hawk say?"

"Oh, we keep that tidbit of information from Hawk. Maverick needs his face to stay pretty."

I laughed. "No doubt."

"Now, it's time for wine."

"Already poured you a glass," Carter said, snagging it from the outdoor table, and handing it to her.

"This is why I love you best."

"Because I do everything in my power to get you drunk?"

"Yes. Absolutely," she said, and stood on her tiptoes to kiss him.

He wrapped an arm around her and pulled her close.

I'd had half a beer and was helping Kim carry dishes to the table when my phone buzzed in my pocket. It was Harmony. I answered immediately. "You okay?"

"No," she whispered. "There was another present."

"You sound freaked."

"It was a dead rat."

My blood ran cold. "Where are you?"

"At the hotel." I heard her sniff, like she was holding back tears.

"Harmony?"

"They left it outside our suite. They know where we are."

"Don't move," I ordered. "And don't touch anything."

"Okay."

I hung up. "Sorry, everyone. I've gotta head out."

"Everything okay?" Kim asked.

"Not sure," I admitted, and grabbed my jacket and keys, heading out the door.

* * *

Harmony

I stood frozen to the floor in the middle of our hotel suite and tried to ignored the gift-wrapped box sitting on the table.

I was currently alone, although, I knew Butchy would be back shortly. We were running a skeleton crew, because he'd sent two of his men with Melody, and Billy and Graham went out for dinner. I had been enjoying an evening alone until Butchy offered to grab Chinese. I hadn't had Chinese in ages, so he'd run out to grab something to eat at a local restaurant.

However, now I wasn't really hungry anymore. Whoever was stalking Melody had left the box not long after he left, and I was just glad she was still out.

The peal of my cell phone pulled me out of my trance and I glanced at the screen. It was Agent Quinn. "Hi."

"You need to buzz me up," Jaxon said, and I nodded even though he couldn't see me.

"I'll come down."

"I don't want you leaving your room, Harmony. Just give permission for me to come up."

"Oh, right. Okay. Um, hold on." I picked up the room phone and gave the concierge what he needed to let Jaxon up, then I went back to Jaxon. "You should be good now."

"I'm stepping into the elevator," he confirmed.

It felt like it took forever for the sound of a knock to come at my door, and I virtually ripped it off its hinges as I pulled it open.

And promptly burst into tears.

"Shit," Jaxon hissed and pulled me against him.

I fisted my hands in his shirt and sobbed into his chest as the past few months of stress flooded me. For the first time since all of this started, someone was listening to me and I hadn't realized how much I'd needed that, until I'd decided to expel all the snot and saliva in my body on his shirt.

He slid a hand to my neck and squeezed gently, rubbing my back with the other. "I got you."

"I was starting to think I was going crazy," I whispered. "I thought I was overreacting."

"You're not overreacting," he assured me.

"I didn't hear anyone in the hallway. Just a

23

knock on the door and then there was the…the package," I hiccupped, pulling away from him. "I thought it was the concierge."

"Okay. We've got security pulling footage from the hallway and the hotel's moving your rooms."

I shook my head and looked up at him. "We should move hotels, don't you think?"

"It's safer to keep you here where we can watch you."

"I'll have Butchy hire a couple more people."

"*I* will take care of that," he countered.

"You can't think it's him. He's been with us for years."

"Harmony, slow down," he said. "You don't need to worry about any of this anymore. I'm gonna have my team take a look at everything and I will make sure you and your sister are safe."

"Harmony?"

I turned to see Butchy walking into the room, his arms laden with food bags. "What the fuck happened?"

I filled him in and he swore.

"Right. We're moving hotels," he said.

"Don't think that's a good idea," Jaxon said.

"Yeah, well you're not their head of security."

"No, but this is now an FBI investigation. I'll be taking it from here." Jaxon focused on me again. "Show me the box."

I pointed to the box on the table. I couldn't make my feet move toward it, and Jaxon didn't make me. He slid on a pair of latex gloves and investigated the box, before pulling out a large plastic bag and slipping the box inside. "I'm gonna take this to my partner, then I'm coming back, okay?"

I nodded, and watched as he walked out the door.

"What happened?" Butchy demanded.

I shrugged. "I'm not entirely sure. Someone left the box with the dead rat in front of the door. I'm assuming it was soon after you left."

He wrapped an arm around me, but I wasn't interested in his touch, so I moved away.

"I don't like this, Harmony," Butchy said, crossing his arms. "Your sister needs to listen to reason."

"I hear you, buddy. But you know what she's like."

He scowled as he pulled out his phone and put it to his ear. "I want her back to the hotel now. I don't give a shit. You have to fuckin' caveman her over your shoulder, you do it. She comes back now. Jesus. Tell her that if she doesn't leave with you now, I'm coming to get her."

I raised an eyebrow. Butchy was acting a little out of character for him, and I wondered what had changed.

"Put her on the phone." He dragged a hand through his hair. "You're back in your room in twenty minutes, Mel, or I'm coming to get you. You don't think? Get your ass back here now. No fuckin' around. We'll explain when you get here. Nineteen minutes, Mel." He hung up without saying goodbye, then focused on me. "No one goes anywhere without me."

I nodded, and he left the room.

My phone buzzed and I answered without looking at the screen. "Hello?"

"It's Jaxon. I'm coming back up."

"Okay," I said, sighing with relief.

I knew I should pull myself together. Remind myself that Jaxon Quinn was an FBI agent investigating a crime. But I couldn't seem to stop my heart from reaching for him. I felt safe and that was an emotion I'd never felt before.

Ever.

I made my way to the door and pulled it open before Jaxon could knock and he cocked his head as he stood in the doorway. "You okay?"

I bit my lip and nodded. "Hmm-mm, come in."

He stepped inside and I closed the door.

"I wasn't expecting you back so quickly."

"Brock came by and picked up the evidence."

"Brock?"

"Part of my team," he explained.

"Oh."

"Harmony, you're white as a sheet. You should probably sit down."

"I'm okay," I lied.

My phone dropped to the floor and I heard Jaxon say, "Shit," as black engulfed me.

Coolness settled on my forehead and I raised my hand to investigate.

"Leave that, Harmony."

I realized relatively quickly that I was stretched out on my sofa, a cold washcloth on my forehead, and Jaxon was sitting beside me, smiling down at me.

"What happened?" I asked.

"You passed out."

I pulled the washcloth off my head and tried to sit up, but Jaxon put his hand on my shoulder. "Stay put."

"I'm fine."

"So fine, you passed out," Jaxon ground out. "Stay put."

"Oh my word, Butchy, calm the hell down,"

Melody snapped as she breezed into the room, stalling when she caught sight of me and Jaxon. Butchy wasn't far behind her, hovering as Melody demanded, "Who are you?"

"I'm Jaxon Quinn," Jaxon said without moving.

"Why are you lying on the sofa?" she asked me.

"Your sister passed out," Jaxon said, his tone one of irritation. "Probably due to stress."

I pushed against him again to sit up. This time he let me. "I'm fine."

"What the hell's going on?" Melody demanded.

"You received a gift. It was a dead rat," I said, matter of factly, standing.

"From whom?" Melody asked.

"We don't know," Butchy said. "But maybe now you'll take this situation seriously."

"Jules—"

"Don't," he warned.

She huffed, making her way to me and pulling me in for a hug. "Are you okay?"

"I'm fine, DiDi. We just need to figure out who's threatening you."

"You and I need to have a conversation," Butchy said, and guided an irritated Melody into her private rooms.

"How long's that been goin' on?" Jaxon asked.

"What?"

He studied me for a few seconds. "How long has your head of security been sleeping with your sister?"

I gasped. "What? He isn't."

"He is."

I stalked to her door and knocked, my heart sinking when it took longer than it should have for my sister to answer it. "Oh, my god," I whispered.

"What's wrong?" Melody asked.

"You and Butchy are sleeping together?"

"What?" she asked, but didn't deny it.

"How long has this been going on under my nose?"

"NiNi—"

I raised my hand, cutting her off. "Don't lie to me."

"Can we please talk about this later?"

"Or never," I said. "I'm done."

"What?"

"I'm done, Melody. I can't do it anymore. I'm out." I shook my head. "Find another idiot to be your scapegoat."

"Harmony, what are you saying?"

"I'm saying I quit. I'm too tired to watch you

29

put yourself into bad situations over and over again. I can't sleep, I've gained, like, twenty pounds from stress, and you don't care. You've never cared. I'm going to call Lyric and have her find you another assistant."

"You just need a break."

"I need to retire," I countered.

"NiNi, I can't do this without you. You know that. Why don't you just take a week? Billy can help me while you're gone."

"Where would I go, Mel?" I asked.

"I know a place," Jaxon said.

"What?" I asked, facing him.

"I know a place you can go where no one will bother you."

"Where?"

"How about I tell you that privately and you can choose whether or not you want to share," he said.

"I accept," I said.

"You don't even know this guy," Melody said.

My mouth dropped open in shock. "Are you seriously saying that to me right now?"

"NiNi."

I ignored her and turned to Jaxon. "I'm packing a bag."

"I'm just gonna make a phone call," he said,

and stepped out of the room.

* * *

Jaxon

I pulled my phone out and called my sister-in-law, hoping my plan wouldn't be thwarted before it was put into action.

"Well, hi there, handsome," she said, and I heard Carter bellow in the background, "Who the fuck are you callin' handsome?"

I grinned. "Hey, Cass. Got a huge favor."

"Lay it on me."

"No one but me's layin' on you, Cass," Carter snapped. "Who the hell is on the phone?"

Cassidy laughed. "It's Jaxon, honey. Keep your pants on."

"Jesus, woman, you're lucky you're cute."

"Ignore him, Jaxon. What do you need?"

I grinned. "How would your parents feel about a visitor for a few days."

"You know they love visitors, especially if it's you."

"Not me. Can't tell you who it is right now, but can you be the buffer and ask them, please?"

"Honey, you know they love you more than me, just call them."

"I'd feel better if you did it."

She sighed. "Okay. Give me five. I'll call

Mom right now."

"Thanks," I said, and we rang off.

I stepped back into Harmony's room just as she dropped a duffle bag on the floor. "I'm ready."

"Are you seriously leaving me here alone?" Melody snapped.

"You're not alone," Harmony countered. "You have a staff of twelve to watch over you."

"God, you're such a fucking selfish cunt!"

I heard Butchy hiss out something unintelligible just as Harmony spun to face her sister with a feral growl. "Excuse me?"

"You heard me."

Harmony squared her shoulders and took a couple of deep breaths. "Thank you, Melody. I appreciate you saying that. Because, at least a cunt is warm and deep. You, on the other hand, are nothing more than a dry, shriveled up, useless vagina! With wrinkles even your botox can't fix."

I tried not to laugh as Melody's hands went to her forehead like she was feeling for nonexistent wrinkles.

"In your vagina!" Harmony added, and scooped up her bag facing me again. "Let's go."

I glanced at Butchy who nodded. Not that I needed his permission or blessing, but if he could keep Melody wrangled, maybe I could keep Harmony from killing her.

I led Harmony from the room and down to the lobby where the concierge was waiting. "I'm so sorry for all the trouble, Miss Morgan."

"I know. I'm going to be out of pocket for a few days. If you need anything, please let Billy know."

"I will, ma'am. Thank you."

I led Harmony to my SUV and helped her inside, then climbed in the front seat, pulling out my phone as I secured my seatbelt. "Hey, Brock. Yeah. Gonna take Melody's sister down to Cass's for a few days. I'll drop her off, then drive back in the morning. Did you get anything on the box?"

"Nothing yet. No fingerprints, but the lab's running it for touch DNA. If you want to stay put down there and see your parents, Dallas and I can dog this. I'll text you if there's anything."

"Yeah?"

"Yeah, brother. You haven't had a day off in over a year. Take a few."

"You got someone on Melody?"

"Yeah. We're working with Butchy to get that covered."

"Okay, man, I appreciate it."

I hung up and started the car...just as Harmony burst into tears.

Shit. I hated it when women cried, but when one so pretty did, it broke my heart.

"I'm sorry, Jaxon," she sobbed out. "I just need a second to process."

I popped open my glove compartment and handed her the box of tissues stored inside. "How about you process with these, and I'll drive?"

She nodded, pulling a wad out of the box. "Thanks."

Cassidy had texted that her parents were happy to host whoever I brought their way, including me. Unfortunately for me, however, my parents lived on the neighboring property, so if I got into town and didn't see them first, I'd hear nothing but grief from my mother. So, I texted her to let her know I'd be visiting for a couple of days, then I pulled onto the freeway and headed south.

Harmony

"HARMONY."

I blinked my eyes open and sat up. "Are we here?"

"Yeah," Jaxon said. "You sure you're okay with this?"

"Yes," I lied. I didn't know these people. I didn't know if they were good or bad, liars or truth-tellers, but right now, they couldn't be any worse than my sister and I needed a fucking break.

"Patrick and Wendy are really good people," Jaxon assured me. "The best."

"They can't be any worse than my sister," I said, then immediately regretted it. "Sorry. That was mean. I actually love my sister. I just don't always like what she does."

"I get it," he said. "Families are complicated."

I shifted to face him. "Why are you doing this?"

He cocked his head. "What do you mean?"

I twisted the tissues in my hands. "Darien called in a favor to get you to look into who was stalking my sister, but you're helping me instead."

"Not instead," he countered. "As well."

I nodded. "As well. I guess I just don't fully understand why."

"Does there need to be a reason outside of it being the right thing to do?"

"No." I shrugged. "I guess I'm just not used to people doing the right thing. The lines have become super blurred and I'm finding it harder to separate the colors."

Jaxon smiled and I swear my panties melted. "Wendy'll help you separate the colors, Harmony. You'll see."

I sighed. "I'm ready."

Jaxon climbed out of the truck, then helped me down and grabbed my bag, carrying it to the front porch. I followed him, the fact that I was walking into a stranger's house just now hitting me.

What the hell am I doing?

"You okay?" he asked.

I realized I'd stopped moving and looked up at Jaxon. "Sorry. Yes."

"I know you don't know me, but Patrick and Wendy are going to make you feel like you're another daughter. You're safe here, Harmony, and I'll be close. If you need me, text me."

"You're staying?"

"My parents live on the property next door."

I glanced around. "Oh, I didn't see any other homes."

"There's over forty acres between."

I bit my lip and nodded. "That makes sense."

"I'll pick you up in the morning and take you to breakfast, sound good?"

"How about lunch? If I'm gonna be able to sleep, I'd actually like to sleep in."

He grinned. "I can do that."

He turned back toward the door, and I reached out and grabbed his arm. "In case I haven't done so already, thank you for going above

37

and beyond. You're incredibly kind, Jaxon."

"You're welcome."

Before we made it to the door, it opened and a beautiful older woman walked out, her hair blonde and curly and she looked like she smiled a lot. "Welcome," she said. "You must be Harmony. I'm Wendy."

"It's wonderful to meet you," I said. "Thank you so much for your hospitality."

"Any friend of Jaxon's is welcome here." Wendy smiled, pulling Jaxon in for a hug. "Especially, if it means we get to see him."

"I'll be here all week," he said. "So, you'll be sick of me before you know it."

"You're staying all week?" I asked.

"Yeah."

"Oh," I whispered, my voice breathy. I cleared my throat and said more confidently, "Cool."

I didn't miss Jaxon raising his eyebrow and giving me a slight smirk, but was able to ignore it since Wendy ushered us inside.

"I'm putting you in Cassidy's old room," Wendy said. "It'll be quiet and you have a private bathroom."

"Thank you."

"Do you have time for a beer?" Wendy asked Jaxon.

He smiled. "Yep. I got all the time in the world."

His smile did things to me. Naughty things, and I knew I needed to get a grip, or I'd kneel before him right here and beg to taste every inch of him.

"You okay?" Jaxon asked, and I blushed sure he could read my mind.

"Yep."

He leaned forward. "You wanna stop biting your lip, Harmony? It's messin' with me."

I gasped quietly and nodded, turning quickly and following Wendy into the kitchen. I heard him chuckle behind me and swallowed to keep myself from sighing out loud.

This was gonna be a big problem for me.

* * *

Jaxon

I reluctantly left Harmony two hours later. Mostly because she could barely keep her eyes open, and I didn't know her well enough to crawl into bed with her.

But it was gonna happen sometime sooner than later, if I had anything to say about it.

Jesus, she was gorgeous. And not just because she was beautiful. She was also funny, thoughtful, and smart. Seemingly, the polar opposite of her sister. Maybe that was ungracious, but the more I heard about Melody, the less I liked her. And that was *after* Harmony made a valiant effort to defend her sister.

How the fuck she could defend her was beyond me, but I kept my mouth shut, and let her fill Wendy and Patrick's heads with bullshit. I was quickly figuring out that Harmony loved her family, almost to distraction, and I wasn't the one to open her eyes to her sister's vapidness.

I climbed into the truck and headed to my parents', wishing I'd stayed at Patrick and Wendy's. I wasn't looking forward to whatever hateful words my mother would passive-aggressively deliver about her daughters-in-law.

Mostly Josh and Carter's wives, to be honest. Melanie and Cassidy, respectively, didn't measure up to Mom's 'standards,' but Kim was revered because she had more money that God. It was disgusting and it was the reason my brothers had cut all ties with her.

Matt, Luke, and I were the holdouts, but, admittedly, I rarely came home because I wasn't interested in hearing the vile things she said. She and I had had multiple conversations on the subject, and I was hoping she'd be a little more gracious this time around.

Pulling up to my parents' home, I parked in front of the garage, taking a deep breath to bolster my patience. I always carried a change of clothes with me, so I grabbed the bag from the trunk and headed inside.

"Oh, honey, you're late," Mom said, rushing into the foyer.

This was the first thing she said to me, indicating this might be a more uncomfortable visit than even I expected. "Sorry, Mom, traffic," I lied as she hugged me.

"There was traffic at Wendy's?"

"Jesus, Mom, you gonna keep bustin' my balls, or are we gonna visit?"

She sighed. "I'm sorry, baby. I just don't understand why you'd stop there first."

"Because I had a package to drop off and it meant I didn't have to come here and then drive back the way I came. Now I can visit with you without interruption."

"Well, there is that," she conceded. "Come in. Are you tired?"

"No, I'm good." I followed her into the kitchen. "Where's Dad?"

"I'm here," he said, pushing up from his recliner and joining us.

I hugged him, noticing he was looking tired. "You okay?"

"Yeah, son. Just dealing with shit at work."

My dad owned a lumber mill and I know he'd been dealing with some bad management. He'd been cleaning up the line of command below him, but it was grueling.

"You gonna join me for a beer?" I asked.

He grinned. "Or twelve."

"One," Mom piped in.

He rolled his eyes making sure she didn't see him, and grabbed us both a beer from the fridge.

The rest of the night was spent in relative ease, mostly because my mother turned in less than an hour after I'd arrived. At almost eleven, I pushed off the sofa and smiled at my dad. "I'm gonna turn in."

"Okay, son. Sleep in tomorrow."

I nodded. "I'm gonna try."

I hugged him and headed up to my childhood room, dropping my bag on the bed. Shit, nothing had changed. My old student-model Squier Stratocaster still hung on the wall and I smiled. I'd long since graduated to collecting vintage Fenders, and my current fixation was a '72 Tele Custom, but I'd never give up my first guitar.

My brothers had all traveled the sports road, mostly football, but I'd always been obsessed with music, and focused all my energy on playing it every second I could. It drove my mom crazy, but Dad would always remind her that I was good at math because of music, so she should be happy.

Our family mill was at the edge of our property, and when we were young, my parents' ran a small dairy farm. I often wondered if it was why they had so many kids…free labor. They sold the cows and some of the land a year or two before Aidan had graduated high school, but kept the mill. Although, Dad had hired a general manager so he could cut back a bit.

It appeared that plan was no longer working.

I pulled my phone out of my pocket and realized it was dead, so I grabbed my charger plugged it in. After powering up my phone again, I saw I'd missed a couple of texts from Harmony and my heart raced a little. Jesus, if she was having a hard time and I wasn't there for her…

Hey, Jax. Thanks for everything. Sleep well.

Then a second text came through.

Sweet dreams.

Then a third.

Sorry, that was weird.

I bit back a chuckle and was about to respond, when another text came through.

Please ignore any strange texts coming from this number. An alien has taken over Harmony's body and is acting the fool.

I pressed the call button and she answered immediately. "Hi, sorry. I thought you'd be asleep."

I smiled. "I don't sleep."

"Neither do I," she admitted.

"You feeling okay?"

"In relation to…?"

"Being at Pat and Wendy's?"

"Oh. Yes. They're amazing."

"So, why can't you sleep?" I asked.

"You don't need to listen to me complain, Jax. I'm sorry. You should—"

"Don't tell me what I should do, Harmony," I countered. "I've been told I'm a good listener, and you sound out of sorts, so if you need to talk, lay it on me."

"It's just that—wait, how would you know if I sounded out of sorts?" she asked.

"Wild guess."

She sighed. "You freak me out, Jaxon."

"Yeah? How so?"

"Because you seem to know things about me even though we've just met," she said. "Is it the profiler in you?"

"Probably." But it wasn't. For whatever reason, I could read her like a book.

"Okay, profiler man, why can't I sleep?"

"First guess would be that your sister's not

looking out for herself, which makes you worry. And even though you two had a blow-out fight and she wasn't particularly kind to you, you're still worried about her."

"Pretty much." Harmony sighed. "I wish I had a bottle of wine."

"Wendy's got a room full of wine."

"I'm not going to ask my hosts if I can drink their wine, Jaxon. That would be rude."

I chuckled. "You want me to bring you some?"

"It's almost midnight."

"So?"

"You'd seriously bring me wine?"

"Yeah. Why not?"

"Lordy, you're sweet."

"Don't tell anyone that," I warned. "I have a reputation to uphold."

She chuckled. "My lips are sealed."

"You want red or white?"

"Oh my word, Jax, no. I'm not making you leave your warm house to bring me booze. If you don't mind taking me to the store tomorrow, I'll grab some then."

"I can do that."

"Thanks. I'm gonna let you go."

"You sure you don't need to talk?"

"If I talk to you right now, I'll cry, and I really don't want to cry."

I scrubbed a hand over my face. "Jesus, Harmony, you're killing me."

"I'm okay. I'm just frustrated and feeling a little off-kilter. I'm not one who likes change, but it's something I'm forced to endure a lot, so I've learned to deal with it. But I don't think I want to do that anymore."

"So, don't."

"Okay," she said, and I heard a smile in her voice. "I'm going to sleep now."

"Good. Call me if you need me."

"I will. Thanks, Jaxon."

"You're welcome, Harmony."

She hung up and I climbed into bed and stared at the ceiling.

FOUR

Harmony

J AXON PICKED ME up the next morning around eleven, and I tried to keep my tongue in my mouth as he slid his hands through his hair. It had started to pour and he'd been caught in it as he made a run from the car to the front door. He wore dark jeans, motorcycle boots, and a black, tight, ribbed Henley under his leather jacket that left nothing to the imagination as to the amount of the muscles underneath.

"Wow, it's crazy right now," I mused, closing the door behind him.

He grinned. "That's pretty mild."

Wendy had stepped into the bathroom and emerged with a towel, handing it to Jaxon.

"Thanks," he said, running it over his head.

"No problem. I've got a fresh pot of coffee on if you want some," Wendy said.

"I'm taking Harmony to lunch, so I'll grab some there."

"Sounds good. I've got some work to do, so I'll see you kids later. You got your key, Harmony?"

I nodded. "Yes, thanks so much."

Wendy walked away and I smiled up at Jaxon. "She gave me a key."

"I heard."

I frowned. "That's weird, right?"

Jaxon shook his head. "Not if you know Wendy."

"Are you sure it's okay?"

"She wouldn't have given you a key if it wasn't," he assured.

"They are so nice."

Jaxon smiled. "Yeah, they are. Salt of earth. Are you ready to go?"

I nodded. I'd worn a pair of dark skinny jeans, knee-high boots, and soft V-neck T-shirt under a tight black hoodie. I had been raised to never leave the house without hair and makeup 'fixed,' and that had been reinforced the second I saw myself in a paparazzi photo after a night of making sure Melody didn't drink herself to death. I'd been dragged out of bed at two a.m., and rushed to a club in midtown New York, dragging her drunk ass out, only to be caught on camera. I looked like the swamp monster, and I swore I'd never let it happen again.

Jaxon led me out to his SUV, holding an umbrella over my head and opening the door for me. I climbed in and he jogged to the driver side, dropping the umbrella in the back before climbing in himself.

"You hungry?" he asked.

"I'm so hungry I could eat the north end of a south-bound goat."

Jaxon laughed. "Then we better get you fed."

As Jaxon drove into the little town, my phone buzzed and I glanced at the screen to see Billy was calling. "Hey, buddy."

"Girl, you need to get back here. Your sister's goin' cray-cray."

"I'm having a time out."

I heard Jaxon chuckle beside me, but ignored him.

"I can't handle her by myself," Billy continued.

"Then take your own time out," I suggested.

"She'd die."

I rolled my eyes. "Well, maybe it's time."

"Jesus," Jaxon hissed beside me and I chanced a glance, seeing him trying to keep himself from laughing.

"Okay, I know you don't mean that," Billy said. "But I get it."

"Is that all?"

"No, it's not all," he whined. "Lyric's flying out."

Okay, this was a surprise, but it was about time, in my opinion. "Well, that's great. She can wrangle Melody. I'm done."

"Oh, my god, are you seriously never coming back?"

I rolled my eyes. "Did I say I was *never* coming back?"

"Well, you didn't tell me when you were coming...or where you are. Where are you?"

I glanced at Jaxon who shook his head.

I bit my lip. "I'm not at liberty to say."

"Girl, I'm about to lose my religion right now."

"Well, you go ahead and do that. I'm going to eat."

"Harmony," Billy growled.

"Billy, seriously, I have to go. I need a break. I'm going to turn my phone off for a few days, okay? I love you, but I really don't want to talk to anyone for a little while."

"Fine," he huffed. "I love you too."

I hung up and shifted to face Jaxon. "You heard all that, huh?"

He smiled. "He's pretty loud. Hard not to."

"This is very true." I bit my lip. "Am I being too hard on him?"

"Are you your sister's keeper?"

"Kind of."

"Legally?" he clarified.

"Well, no."

"Is she a grown-ass adult woman?"

"Depends on the day," I retorted.

He grinned. "You deserve a break, Harmony. Sounds like your other sister's gonna come take some of the burden off your shoulders, so let her do that."

"LiLi's going to freak."

"LiLi?"

"Lyric. I'm NiNi, Melody's DiDi, and so on." I sighed. "It's silly."

"I think it's sweet."

"You do?"

"Yeah, but don't tell anyone."

"Street cred?" I deduced.

"Sure, we'll go with that." He laughed and turned off the truck. "Don't move."

I waited while he grabbed the umbrella and walked to my side of the truck and helped me down. Once I was out and under the protection of the umbrella, he led me to a little café on the corner of the gorgeous downtown area that spanned about two blocks. "It's so pretty here. It reminds me of home."

"Yeah?" Jaxon asked, as he held the door and shook out the umbrella.

"Yes. Very old-timey," I said, and stepped inside. "I'm kind of a sucker for history."

"Me too."

"Really?"

He nodded. "It's why I do what I do."

"Lyric restored her 1860 home near Forsyth Park and Melody and I both have rooms there for holidays. It's gorgeous."

"I'd love to see it some time."

"I'd love to show it to you," I admitted.

"Jaxon Quinn, honey, as I live and breathe!" an older woman called out.

Jaxon turned toward her and she rushed over, wrapping her arms around his waist.

He hugged her back and chuckled. "Ms. Peggy, how are you?"

"Still breathing."

"You look exactly the same."

"Charmer." She smacked his chest. "Who's your friend?"

"Harmony, this is Peggy. She and her husband have run the café since I was...well, before I was."

I smiled and shook her hand. "It's nice to meet you."

"You too, honey. Why do you look familiar?"

My heart raced. "Um…"

"I'll fill you in later, if that's okay," Jaxon said to Peggy. "But it'd be great if you didn't see us."

Peggy smiled. "My lips are sealed. Now, you kids sit anywhere. I'll bring you a couple of menus."

Jaxon guided us to a booth away from the windows and we sat facing each other.

"Why did you go into the FBI?" I asked.

"Not sure there was a specific reason. Just kind of fell into it. My brother was first, then I met my crew in the academy and we all went for it together."

"Your crew?"

"My brother, Matt, runs a team of six, including Me, Brock, and Dallas. You'll probably meet

them in the coming days. They're working behind the scenes to get your situation worked out."

"So, it's kind of a family thing?"

Jaxon chuckled. "Well, no. There are six of
us"

"Wait, really?"

He nodded.

"Are you religious?" I asked.

Jaxon let out a snort. "Not even close."

Peggy dropped a couple of menus off, after
pouring Jaxon a cup of coffee. I ordered a coke
and she left us to look over the food options.

"So, not religious…" I prompted.

"*So* not religious," he confirmed with a grin.
"Josh is married with kids, he's a CPA, Matt and
I are FBI, Luke's still figuring out what he wants
to do, but working construction in the meantime,
then Carter and Aidan are both part of an MC.
Aidan's a vet, Carter's a mechanic."

"MC?"

"Motorcycle club."

"Wait, really? How does that work with two
brothers being in law-enforcement?" I closed my
menu, knowing exactly what I wanted.

"They're not a 1% club," Jaxon said, dropping his menu on top of mine.

"That's the illegal kind, right?"

"Right."

"Wow," I breathed out.

Peggy returned to take our order and I chose a burger with everything, including a chocolate milkshake.

"I'll have what she's having," Jaxon said. "I'm good with the coffee, though."

"Which one's the vet?" I asked.

"Aidan. His club name's Knight."

"Because he's dark or because he's a hero?" I asked.

Jaxon's mouth turned up in a slight smirk. "Very astute. Definitely the hero kind. He trains horses as well. His wife, Kim, won Olympic gold in Rio under his tutelage."

"Shut up, really?"

He nodded. "She's kind of badass."

"Sounds like it."

"Your turn," he said.

"My turn?"

"How did you get roped into being Melody's punching bag."

"She wasn't always like this," I admitted. "Believe it or not, she was the sweet one."

"I'll take your word for it."

Peggy delivered my milkshake and I leaned back in my seat. "It started out as the three of us. We were a family act and did everything together, but then a skeevy manager told my mother Melody was the cash cow and would make her millions, and the rest is history. Lyric went on to law school and I followed Melody. I got my degree online for the most part, so it took a little longer than I liked. But I just felt like I couldn't leave her alone with our mother, and then when Mom died, I was so far in, I didn't feel like I had any other discernable skills, if that makes sense."

"Yeah it makes sense. But your skills are exceedingly apparent to me, even if you don't see them."

I smiled. "Thanks. I've been so focused on my sister, I've let that side of my life lapse. Which is sad, because my mom created a monster. I hate to say that, because I love my sister, but she's spiraling. And I think she's self-medicating with more than alcohol, although, I haven't been able to find out what she's taking." I shrugged. "I just need a break."

"And you're getting one," Jaxon reminded me, gently.

I sighed. "Yes. I need to be in the moment and enjoy it."

I took a long sip of the milkshake and grinned.

"Do you still sing?"

"Sometimes. I don't get to do it as much, just

because we never have time, but I drag my acoustic out of its case on occasion and get lost in the moment," I admitted. "I really miss my piano, but it's not as easy to carry an upright around. What about you? Are you musical?"

"Yeah. I play a little guitar and have been known to sing."

"Do you have a guitar with you?"

He cocked his head. "At my parents' place, yeah. Why?"

"Just wondering," I said, sipping my milkshake again.

"I'll make you a deal."

"Okay."

"I drag my old guitar out of hiding, you sing for me."

"Only if you join me," I challenged.

"We'll see."

"Those are my terms," I insisted.

Before he could agree or disagree, Peggy arrived with our food, and we got down to eating.

* * *

Jaxon

I'd never seen a woman inhale food the way Harmony did, and it was a strange turn-on for me. I'd always been attracted to women with a little meat on their bones, and Harmony didn't disappoint.

"Do I have something on my face?" Harmony asked, dropping a fry and wiping her mouth with a napkin.

"No, why?"

"You're staring at me."

I smiled. "You're easy to look at."

"Okay, Romeo." She rolled her eyes. "Seriously, though."

"Honestly? I like that you're eating like a real woman."

"What's that supposed to mean?"

Her question sounded barbed, but her tone indicated she was genuinely interested. "I've always been a little suspicious of women who only eat kale."

She let out a quiet but fucking adorable little snort. "I will *never* eat kale on purpose. Kale is disgusting. As is quinoa, tofu, and anything gluten free."

I grinned. "I knew there was a reason I liked you."

I heard her quick inhale, then she started to cough uncontrollably and I suddenly felt like an ass. "Shit," I hissed, sliding from the booth to get to her.

She waved her hand dismissively, holding

her palm up to ward me off. "I'm okay," she choked out, then coughed a little more, chugged some water, then coughed again. "I'm okay, Jax. You can sit down. I'm not going to die."

I smiled. "Well, the coughing indicated there was no chance of death, but I wanted to be ready just in case."

"Warn me when you're gonna flirt with me," she demanded.

"You think that was flirting?"

Her cheeks pinkened. "Wasn't it?"

"Baby, if I was gonna flirt, you'd know it."

"Calling me 'baby' isn't really the best way to convince me you're not flirting, FYI."

She had me there.

Jesus, she was gorgeous.

"Sorry, Harmony. I don't mean to make you feel uncomfortable."

"Oh, you don't," she said. "Different time, different place, you'd already be naked and I'd be using you for all manner of guilty pleasures."

"Fuck," I breathed out, then burst out laughing. "Payback's a bitch."

She smiled slowly. "It's cute you think I'm kidding."

That shut me up real quick. "You're not?"

"Hell, no." She leaned forward. "I like sex,

Jaxon. Love it, actually. So, so much. Unfortunately, I'm in the middle of a really long dry spell, so you say the word, and I'll let you be the farmer who waters my crops."

I felt the zipper of my jeans get tight and I shifted slightly to ease the ache. "Don't typically fuck and run, Harmony."

"Well, that's good to know. Running while fucking can be pretty messy, not to mention dangerous. You could put an eye out."

"Jesus," I hissed on a laugh. "You can't say shit like that to me in public."

She shrugged, wiping her hands. "Am I currently under your protection? By that I mean, are you working…am I your responsibility?"

"No." I smiled. "Technically, I'm on vacation."

"Well, there you have it. So am I. You just let me know, Romeo. I'm in if you are."

"I'm a red-blooded, American man, and you're hot as fuck," I whispered. "You think I want to turn that down?"

"I'm kind of hoping you won't. And I'm really hoping you know a place we can go right now."

"That'll be a bit of a challenge, but you give me a little time, and I'll make it happen."

"Did I mention it's been a long time?"

Jesus, this woman was killing me. "Yeah, baby, you mentioned that."

She smiled. "Good."

I was gonna have to find somewhere private soon.

* * *

Harmony

Oh, my god, I couldn't believe I'd just done that! I had never offered myself up for sex to anyone, let alone a virtual stranger. And that dry spell? It had been more than two years because my last boyfriend decided he was more interested in Melody than me.

But there was something about Jaxon Quinn I couldn't resist. I wanted to know what it felt like to be fucked until I couldn't walk straight, and I just knew Jaxon would be the man to do that. I wouldn't leave him with any strings tied to me. Once Melody's shooting schedule was done, we'd go home and Jaxon would go about his life.

It would be perfect and I couldn't wait.

FIVE

Harmony

TWENTY MINUTES, JAXON texted and my heart raced.

Okay, no, it was more like my lady bits raced. Or zinged. Or raced *and* zinged. Oh, my god, I was swampy just thinking about Jaxon getting into my pants.

It was about eleven a.m., I was at Wendy and Patrick's, already showered and dressed appropriately for a clandestine sex rendezvous with the object of my desire, and I couldn't wait to get the hell out of here.

I had taken time in the shower to shave all the applicable spots that should be hairless, and managed to do it without bloodshed. I did a quick pit sniff test and determined I smelled just the right amount of flowery, so now I was just waiting for Jaxon to get here.

Grabbing my purse, I headed downstairs. Patrick was at work and Wendy was out running errands, so I had the house to myself for the moment. Which made the waiting worse, to be honest. I started to think of all the reasons I shouldn't do this and it was drowning out the voice of insanity. I didn't want to hear reason. I wanted to throw caution to the wind for once in my life.

Before I could talk myself out of what I knew would be an incredible sexual encounter, the doorbell rang and I was rushing to the door.

I pulled it open and bit my lip so hard, it almost bled. God, he was edible. Dark jeans, cowboy boots this time, and a tight, blue button up showcased his big chest. I couldn't wait to peel him out of every stitch.

"Hey," he said, his voice low and sexy.

"Hi." I smiled. "Are you ready?"

"Yeah, Harmony, I'm ready. Are you?"

I nodded.

"Come on, then."

I nodded again and locked up the house before following him to the truck. He held the door for me and climbed inside. He made his way to the driver's side and started the engine.

"Condoms!" I blurted.

"Got that covered, Harmony," Jaxon said.

I blushed. "Oh, right. Okay, thanks."

Jaxon reached over and took my hand. "You can say no at any point."

"I'm not going to say no."

"Just putting it out there. You can stop this even if we've started."

"I have no plans to stop anything. Unless you suck."

"Excuse me?"

I met his eyes. "If you don't make me come—"

He laughed. "You're gonna come, Harmony. More than once. That I can promise you."

I shivered and Jaxon backed out of the driveway.

We drove for about five minutes in total silence and just as I was about to babble incoherently to make myself feel better, Jaxon pulled up to a huge red barn. It was the quintessential American farm sight. "A barn?"

"Trust me," he said, turning off the engine.

"As long as you're not gonna fuck me on a

hay bale, I'm good."

Jaxon laughed and once we'd climbed out of the truck, he took my hand and led me inside. I saw six stalls, although, there were currently no horses in them, and to the right of the double sliding doors was a staircase.

"Up here," Jaxon said, and we climbed the steps. He pulled out a key and unlocked and opened the door, pushing it open and tugging me inside.

"Oh, wow," I breathed out.

This must have been a caretaker's residence. There was a small living room which was open to a kitchen divided by a surprisingly large island.

"This is so cute."

"Yeah," he said distractedly. "Follow me."

We walked down a short hallway, past a bathroom, and into a bedroom that had a queen-sized bed and a small dresser.

Jaxon dropped his keys on the dresser and faced me. "If you want to stop, just say the word."

I nodded, and he slid his hand to my neck, stroking my jaw. "You're beautiful, Harmony, and I'm not just saying that because we're about to make some magic."

I grinned. "Back atya."

His lips settled on mine, gently at first, but when I opened my mouth for him, our kiss became frantic. We were all lips and tongues and I could *not* get enough.

"Jesus," Jaxon hissed out. "We need to slow down."

"Do we?" I challenged.

He smiled. "I'm on your time, Harmony, so it's your call."

My hands went to the buttons of his shirt and I forced myself not to tear them from the material. "I want to see you."

He made quick work of his shirt and slid it off and I gasped quietly at the sight of his chest. No tattoos, muscles upon muscles, and he obviously waxed. I leaned forward and ran my tongue between the groove of one of his abs, and found myself lifted and dropped onto the bed.

"I was enjoying that," I complained.

He grinned. "You can have more later," he promised, unzipping my boots and sliding them off my feet.

He moved up my body, unbuttoning my jeans and kissing my belly just above the waistband of my panties.

"Lift," he directed, and I lifted my hips so he could tug my jeans from my thighs. He left my panties where they were, but threw my jeans in

66

the corner. I started to sit up, but his hand settled gently on my stomach. "Don't move."

I flopped back down with a sigh.

"Patience, Harmony."

"A virtue that isn't mine," I retorted.

He chuckled, leaning down to kiss my belly, pushing my shirt up. "Slide your hands above your head."

I did as he directed and he slid my shirt toward my wrists, tying it around my arms, tight enough to make things interesting.

"Too tight?" he asked.

"No," I rasped.

I'd worn a front snap bra and was glad I had, as Jaxon made quick work of undoing it, freeing my breasts and burying his face between them.

I squirmed as he drew one nipple into his mouth and sucked gently, then took the other one and did the same. "Fuckin' beautiful," he said.

I smiled. I let his words wash over me. I had great boobs, I knew that, and I owned it. It was my thighs I wasn't a particular fan of, but I hoped he'd be too distracted to pay attention to them. He kissed his way back down my belly and dipped his tongue just under my panty line, before sliding my underwear off my body.

Kneeling between my legs, Jaxon pushed my thighs apart and I squeezed my eyes shut.

"Look at me, Harmony," he ordered.

I forced my eyes open, and the look on his face was confusing. Concern mixed with lust. "What?"

"Why are you hiding from me?" he asked.

"What do you mean?"

"You're shutting down."

"I am not."

He frowned. "Baby, you closed your eyes and your body stiffened."

I bit my lip. Shit. He was right. "I'm not shutting down. Not really," I countered.

"Then why are you tensing up?"

"I don't know," I lied, closing my eyes again.

I felt him leave me briefly, opening my eyes again to watch as he stretched out beside me. His jeans were still on, but he'd removed his boots. "What are you doing?"

"We're gonna talk," he said, settling his head in his palm.

"That wasn't the deal."

He smiled. "Harmony, you're not going to enjoy this if you can't relax."

"I'm relaxed. So totally relaxed," I said, reaching out to touch his chest and remembering I was still tied. I freed myself and rolled onto my side, mirroring his position, running a finger over his chest briefly, just because I had to. "I'll do better."

"Harmony, you're not doing anything wrong, I just want to understand what's in your head."

"I'm not paying attention to what's in my head, so you shouldn't either," I argued. "How about you worry about what's in my vagina? I'd very much like your dick to pay attention to that."

He chuckled. "You being cute isn't going to stop this process."

"I don't get you," I complained, flopping onto my back and dragging my hands down my face.

"What's not to get?"

"I'm naked here, ready and willing, and you want to 'talk.' Why won't you just be a typical guy and fuck me already?"

"Because I want you to enjoy it too."

"I will!" I promised.

His hand cupped my breast and I realized far too late that I froze.

"Yeah, I can tell," he said.

I pushed off the bed with a frustrated growl. "It's only because you've gotten in my head."

He sat up and settled his elbows on his knees. "Don't get me wrong, I'm all in, but in order for me to enjoy this, I need you to have fun. So tell me why you're all locked up."

I paced the small room. "I just wanted a one-night—no, a one-day stand. I wasn't expecting to deal with *feelings,*" I hissed, snagging my clothes off the floor. "Go ahead and take me back to Wendy's. This was obviously a dumb idea."

Jaxon slid off the bed and took my clothes from my hands. "It wasn't a dumb idea."

"Then, what was it?"

He smiled. "A chance to blow off some steam, which is always a *great* idea."

I sighed. "Except, I couldn't even do that right."

Dropping my clothes back on the floor, he cupped my face. "You're not doing anything wrong, Harmony," he repeated. "We're getting to know each other. I'm not going anywhere, so just take your time and if it doesn't happen, it's okay."

"But I don't want to be a cock tease."

"Well, technically, wouldn't you be a crop tease?"

"Oh, my god," I bit out as I forced back a laugh and dropped my forehead to his chest. "I was not expecting you, Jaxon Quinn."

He stroked my hair. "You took the words right out of my mouth."

I met his eyes. "I may have told you a little

lie."

"Yeah?"

I nodded. "I'm not really all that confident about sex. I mean, I think I like it, I just haven't really enjoyed it with anyone other than my vibrator," I whispered, then immediately added, "Jesus, why the hell did I just tell you that?"

His lips settled on mine and I slid my hands around his waist as he kissed me gently. "Fuck, you're gorgeous," he rasped, breaking the connection.

"So are you."

He kissed me again and I melted into him. The second my nipples connected with his chest, they pebbled into tight peaks. I shifted to cause a little more friction, and whimpered against his mouth as my body zinged at the sensation.

"You okay?" he panted out.

"God, yes. Don't stop."

He kissed me again, lifting me so I could wrap my legs around his waist, then carried me back to the bed.

Making quick work to remove the rest of our clothing, he knelt between my legs again and covered my core with his mouth. I slid my fingers into his hair and arched into his mouth, whimpering with need as his tongue dipped inside of me.

He slipped a finger inside of me, then another as he continued to work my clit with his mouth. I felt the pressure build inside of me and as much as I wanted the ecstasy to last, my body had other ideas, and I cried out as a climax washed over me.

Before I could completely come down, Jaxon rolled on a condom and slipped inside of me. I wrapped my legs around his waist, and drew him deeper as he bit down gently on my nipple. The sensation shot through my body and I arched against him, trying to get closer.

Jaxon's big hands linked with mine and he dragged them over my head, immobilizing me as he thrust into me, slowly at first, then faster. I could feel another orgasm building and I whispered, "Get there," and anchored a foot to the bed so I could meet each thrust with one of my own.

Oh, my god, his chest hit my breasts as he thrust harder and I could no longer hold back my climax. "Now!" I cried out, my walls contracting around Jaxon's dick as my body shuddered in release.

Jaxon let out a quiet grunt and I felt him pulse inside of me as he kissed me deeply and rolled us on our sides facing each other. "Holy shit," he panted out.

"I'm so sorry, Jax. I wasn't expecting that to happen so fast."

He grinned, kissing me again, quickly, but sweetly. "That was fucking amazing, Harmony. Don't ever apologize to me when you're naked."

"What if I accidentally knee you in the family jewels?"

"Don't even need to apologize then, if you're naked."

"What if I elbow you in your nose?"

"Are you naked?"

"Sure, in this scenario, yes, I'm naked."

"You don't need to apologize."

"Umm, what if I slam my head into yours...accidentally, of course."

"Again. Are you naked?"

"Yes."

"You don't need to apologize," he repeated.

I smiled. "What if I'm not naked?"

"Then you need to apologize."

"So, what I'm hearing you say, is that as long as you see the titties and bury yourself deep inside the lady bits, I can do anything to you without consequence."

He chuckled, kissing me again. "Pretty much."

"You're like the perfect guy," I said in a sing-song voice.

"I'm aware. I'm the whole fucking package," he retorted, sliding out of me. "I'm gonna get rid of the condom."

I watched him walk away, but he returned quickly, and slid back into bed, pulling me against his chest.

Rain was coming down in sheets outside as I snuggled close. "How did you know about this place?"

"My parents' own it. Up until a few years ago, Aidan kept horses downstairs and lived up here."

"No more horses, huh?" I asked.

"He and his wife, Kim, own property in Portland, so they keep their horses there now."

"Oh, wow. Still, even if no one lives here, it's so clean."

His hand stroked my back. "That's because I cleaned it."

"You did? When?"

"This morning. I came by and did a quick clean and changed the sheets."

I smiled, kissing his chest. "You did a great job."

He chuckled. "I was motivated."

"Apparently," I said. "I really enjoyed this, Jax. Thanks."

He wrapped my hair around his hand and tugged gently. "You sound like it's never going to happen again."

"It's not." I met his eyes. "Is it?"

"I'd like it to. You?"

I bit my lip. "I'm going home. There's no point in starting something we can't finish."

"When do you go home?"

"About a month. As soon as the movie's done."

"So, let's have some fun for 'about a month,'" he said.

"Are you okay with being exclusive for a month? I don't really like to share." Jesus, I was seriously bold with this man. I had never said anything like this to anyone, let alone a man I was interested in.

He grinned. "Yeah, baby, I'm good with being exclusive."

"How many women are going to be upset by that?"

"Oh, all of them," he said.

I bit back a wave of jealousy and dropped my head back on his chest. "Right. Of course."

His body shook as he chuckled. "And by all of them, I mean, none."

"Oh," I whispered, and Jaxon rolled me onto my back, hovering above me.

"Haven't fucked anyone in over a year."

"How come?" I blurted.

"Haven't found anyone I was interested in." He smiled. "Until you."

"Seriously?"

"Seriously." He kissed me, then ran his nose against mine. "What about you?"

"I'm practically a monk."

"You on the pill?"

"Yes. I have bad periods," I said. "Not that you needed to know that."

"I'll get tested."

"Why?"

"So we don't have to use a condom."

"Oh, right." I squeezed my eyes shut. "Makes sense."

"Are you okay with that?"

"Yes."

"You sure?"

I looked up at him. "Yes, why do you keep asking?"

"Because you got all stiff again, and not in a good way."

I sighed. "Are you like this with every woman you sleep with?"

"What way?"

"Clairvoyant."

His mouth twitched. "No."

"I find that hard to believe."

He stroked my cheek, running his thumb gently over my bottom lip. "I've never had a one-night stand, and I've never slept with anyone after only knowing them a day."

"Great, I'm a slut," I grumbled.

"If you're a slut, then I am too."

I couldn't stop a grin. "I'm okay with that, if we're in this together."

He kissed me again. "We're totally in this together."

I sighed. "I really like you, Jaxon."

"What a coincidence," he said. "I really like me too."

I laughed, shaking my head. "Your parents really sucked at giving you self-esteem."

"Oh, I know. I have always threatened to send them my therapy bills." He settled back on the bed and pulled me over his chest. "In all seriousness, though. I really like you too, Harmony. I like the idea of getting to know you over the next few weeks."

His phone buzzed on the nightstand and he grabbed it, keeping me tight to his body. "Hey, Brock. Yeah?" Releasing me, he sat up. "Nothing? Hmm. Yeah, that's interesting. Yep, it's what I'm thinking too. Sure. Okay. We'll talk tomorrow. Bye." Jaxon set his phone back on the nightstand and shifted to face me.

"What?" I asked, sitting up, my heart racing. "Is Mel okay?"

"She's fine. In fact, she's perfectly safe."

"Okay." I relaxed. "Then why do you look concerned?"

"Not sure yet."

"What aren't you telling me?"

"I don't think your sister's the target."

"What the hell does that mean?" I asked, sitting up on my knees.

He sighed. "I think you're the target."

"What the—? Um, no. There's no way. I'm a nobody."

"Nobodies get stalked all the time," he pointed out.

I slid off the bed and grabbed my clothes. "What evidence do you have?"

"Years of tracking down psychos who disobeyed restraining orders."

"No," I snapped. "That it's me that's being stalked."

His mouth went up in a smirk, indicating he knew exactly what I was asking. "It's a theory right now."

"Well, your theory's wrong." I pulled my T-shirt on over my head.

"Where are you going?" he asked.

"Don't we need to head back?"

"Not if we don't want to." He patted the mattress. "We can even stay all night."

I shook my head. "I'd like to go back to
Wendy's."

"Okay." He sighed as he stood and got
dressed without comment.

Harmony

W E DROVE BACK to Patrick and Wendy's in silence. Me lost in my thoughts, and Jaxon leaving me to them. There was no way I was the target of whatever this was. I didn't interact with anyone other than our staff and venue manager-types, and I made damn sure I was out of sight. I didn't even go to the set when Melody was filming. *My* assistant acted as her PA as far as the public was concerned.

We pulled up the long driveway and Jaxon parked the SUV, reaching over and taking my hand. "We're gonna figure this out. You and your sister are both safe in the meantime."

"It's not me," I said. "It's really not."

He smiled gently. "Put it out of your mind. My team has your sister covered, and I've got you, okay?"

"Maybe I should go back."

"No," he said quicker than I liked.

"Why not? I'm not the one in danger," I insisted.

He sighed. "Look. We've just had the greatest afternoon I can recall in a while, can we maybe repeat that a few more times before we have to get back to reality?"

"A few more times?" I repeated.

"Yes."

"That's more than twice."

Jaxon grinned. "Generally, yes."

I raised an eyebrow. "You think you can do it more than twice?"

"I have no idea." He laughed. "But I'm willing to try if you'll let me."

"Is Melody really okay?"

"Yes." He squeezed my hand. "And she will

continue to be. Trust me."

"Will you take me back to that diner for a shake?"

"Yeah, tonight if you want."

"And a burger?"

He nodded. "You can even have fries *and* tots."

"Oh, wow. Fries *and* tots? That's so generous."

"I'm a giver."

"Yeah, you are," I deadpanned.

He laughed again, climbing out of the SUV and walking to my side, helping me down. He walked me to the door and kissed me gently. "Pick you up at six."

"Okay."

"Pack a bag and we'll stay in the barn."

"You're so romantic."

He nodded. "If you're lucky, I'll find one of Aidan's old whips. I'll show you romance like you've never seen."

I snorted on a laugh. "Just don't replace the bed with bales of hay."

"I can do that." He stroked my cheek. "Six."

"Okay."

I let myself in and locked the door behind me not sure if I was more excited by the sex, or the fries and tots.

* * *

Jaxon

I left Harmony at the Dennis home, then headed back to my parents', calling Brock on the way.

"Hey, brother," Brock said.

"Hey. What did you find?"

"Nothing."

"At all?"

"Exactly," he said.

"Which indicates Melody isn't the target," I deduced. "*Or*, the person could be using Harmony's absence to make us think that."

Brock sighed. "Yeah. I'm not liking this."

"Me neither."

"Matt wants you to stay put for the moment."

My phone buzzed and I glanced at the screen. "That's him calling now."

Brock chuckled. "I'll let you go."

"Thanks. We'll talk tomorrow."

"Sounds good."

Brock hung up and I answered my brother's call. "Hey."

"Hey, little brother, how's Mom?"

"Behaving herself for the moment."

"Shit. Seriously?"

"So far," I confirmed.

"Jesus, you really are the mom whisperer."

I chuckled. "Maybe so."

"Did Brock fill you in?"

"Yeah. I'm supposed to stay put for a bit, huh?"

"Yeah. You okay with that? I can send Miller down if need be."

There was no way in hell I was letting Nolan Miller anywhere near Harmony. "Nah, it's all good. She's happy at the Dennis', and I figure I'll take one for the team in regards to Mom."

Matt laughed. "You always were the selfless one."

"Sure, we can go with that."

"Is she a nightmare?"

"Who?" I asked. "Harmony?"

"Yeah. I can't imagine two like Melody in the world, but if she's even half the pain in the ass, then I'm sorry."

I chuckled. "She's nothing like Melody, actually. Totally down to earth."

"Well, if that changes and you're done with it all, just say the word. I'll send Miller."

No way in hell. "Okay, brother, I appreciate it."

"Talk to you later."

My brother hung up and I headed into the house, my phone buzzing just as I removed my jacket. It was Harmony and I couldn't stop a smile. "Miss me already?"

"I need you to come back," she whispered frantically, and my blood froze.

"You okay?" I asked as I rushed back to the truck.

"Someone's here," she whispered. "And it's not Patrick or Wendy. They're moving around the house."

"Where are you?"

"I'm hiding in the closet."

"I'm on my way, don't hang up."

"Okay," she whispered.

I had just pulled into the driveway when I heard Harmony scream and then the line went dead.

* * *

Harmony

I dropped my phone just as a banshee came at me with flailing arms, nails, and the voice from hell. I fought back with everything I had, certain I was done for.

"Freeze!" Jaxon bellowed from somewhere close and the banshee squeaked in fright, but stopped her attack. "Jesus. Mia?"

"What the hell are you doing here, Jax?" Mia demanded. "And who the hell are you?"

This question was directed at me. "I'm Harmony."

"She's staying with your parents for a few days," Jaxon provided, sliding his gun back in his holster. I inched my way toward him, trying to get away from the crazy lady.

"Well, that would have been stellar information to know," Mia snapped.

"Harmony, this is Mia. She's one of Cassidy's sisters. Actually, she's the certifiable one."

"Fuck you, Jax. Nothing has ever been certified in writing or otherwise," she retorted, but her mouth twitched up in a smile. "I'm really sorry for going all kung fu fighting on you, but I couldn't figure out who the hell would be hiding in my sister's closet."

I felt Jaxon's hand settle on my lower back and I leaned into it. "It's all good. It's nice to meet you."

"What are you doing here, Mia? I thought you were in Seattle," Jaxon said.

"Nah, I'm over that fucking city. I'm home for a few days."

"Do your parents know you're home?"

She crossed her arms. "I was going to surprise them."

Jaxon grinned. "Pretty sure you'll do that in

spades."

"Why do you look familiar?" Mia asked me.

"Probably because I look like my sister."

"Oh, yeah? Who's your sister?"

I leaned further into Jaxon's hand needing his comfort. "Melody Morgan."

"Holy shit, seriously?" She wagged her finger at Jaxon. "Now, that's someone who's certifiable."

"Jesus, Mia," Jaxon growled.

Mia grimaced. "No offense, Harmony."

"None taken," I said. I heard my phone buzz from the closet and rummaged inside, finding it in the corner. "Hello?"

"Bitch, where the hell are you?" Melody snapped.

"None of your business."

"You need to come back."

"No," I said firmly.

"Lyric is arriving tomorrow morning and I will *not* be left alone with her."

I rolled my eyes. "She's our big sister, DiDi, not some monster."

"She's always trying to censor me," she whined. "And control my freedom. If you don't come back immediately, I'll fire you."

"Do it," I challenged. "I haven't had a vacation in five years, so fire me and I'll slap a wrongful termination suit on you so fast, your head will spin."

"You wouldn't dare."

"I'm no longer willing to put up with your manipulation, baby sister, so feel free to suck it, then after you've done that, why don't you go ahead and fuck the fuck off?" I hung up and stepped out of the closet, stalling at the expression on Mia's face.

She doubled over, bursting into uncontrollable laughter. "Oh, my god, I think you just became my new best friend."

While Mia continued laughing like a loon, Jaxon frowned and mouthed, *"You okay?"*

I shook my head, biting back tears. God, I was tired.

"Mia, give us a minute, would you?"

Mia waved her hand, still laughing, and walked out of the room.

Jaxon closed the distance between us and pulled me against his body. "I'm so tired, Jaxon. Tired of her manipulation. Tired of not putting down roots. Tired of her nagging at me every second of every day." I burrowed into his chest, wrapping my arms around his waist. "I just want to go home."

He slid a hand into my hair and massaged my scalp. "How about you give me your phone and we ignore any phone calls for a while?"

"Okay."

"Um, guys?" Mia called. "I think we've got a problem."

"What?"

"I just got accosted by a reporter at the front door. I slammed it on her face, but there's more in the way of news crews and paparazzi making their way up our driveway."

"Fuck," he snapped, and released me. "Stay put."

I nodded, sitting on the edge of the bed and dropping my face into my hands.

What now?

I waited in the bedroom for close to ten minutes before Jaxon came back and knelt in front of me. "Someone tipped the paparazzi off that Melody Morgan was here."

"My sister did that to get back at me."

"Yes," Jaxon said. "Brock said she confessed."

"That bitch," I hissed.

"We're gonna need to find another place to lay low."

I bit my lip. "The barn?"

"Yeah, if you're okay with that."

"For how long?" I asked, secretly hoping he'd say forever.

"Until they get bored and give up."

I squeezed my eyes shut and nodded. "They're vultures."

"Indeed."

"How are we going to get out of here?"

"Mia's got a plan, so pack your bag and we'll get out of here."

I sighed. "I'll be quick."

"Okay. Meet me downstairs."

Jaxon left me and I went about packing up my meager belongings.

* * *

Twenty minutes later, we were on an ATV heading through the back of the Dennis property toward the Quinn barn.

In the pouring rain.

By the time Jaxon pulled the ATV into the barn, we were both soaked. I climbed off the vehicle and removed my helmet, wiping my face and trying to keep from freezing.

"Jesus, now I feel less like Kim Possible and more like Rufus the naked mole rat."

Jaxon pulled his helmet off and set it on the seat. "I don't know anything about Kim Possible or mole rats, but I'd sure love to see you naked again, so let's get you out of those wet clothes, huh?"

"Oh, now I see why you were so eager to get

back here."

He chuckled. "Busted."

He grabbed my bag and followed me up the stairs, letting us inside the tiny apartment.

I rubbed my hands, blowing on them in an effort to get warm.

"Go take a shower," Jaxon said. "I'll get the fire started."

I almost kissed him for his kindness, but I was way too cold, so I grabbed my bag and headed to the bathroom. It was small, but it looked like it had been updated recently, and the water pressure was awesome, so I lingered.

"You ever coming out?" Jaxon called.

I'd apparently lingered a little too long.

"I haven't decided yet," I retorted, but turned off the water anyway.

I dried off and pulled on some clean clothes, then headed out to the living room where Jaxon had a roaring fire happening in the wood stove in the corner. "Oh lordy, that's nice."

Jaxon grinned from his place at the small kitchen island. "Yeah. Wine?"

"Oh, yes, please. Wait. Where did you get wine?"

"Mia loaded us up with a few things. She's heading to the store to stock her parents' back up. We have enough food for dinner tonight and breakfast. We can head to Pixie's tomorrow for more provisions."

"Pixie's?"

"Local grocer." He handed me a glass of wine. "I figured it'll be safer than heading to Freddies the next town over."

"The second they figure out it's not Melody, they'll be gone. We can probably go wherever we want."

"Let's hope," he said. "We're gonna need to do something with your phone, Harmony. Your sister tracked you and I don't like that."

I sighed. "I turned it off, but I get it."

"All communication should go through me from this point forward. If you need to talk to anyone, I'll call whoever's on watch."

"Is your phone not trackable?"

"Not by anyone other than law enforcement."

I smiled. "Show off."

He chuckled. "Yeah. You hungry?"

"Starving."

"Can you cook?" he asked, hopefully.

"Yep."

"Do you like to cook?" he continued.

"Love it."

"So…?"

I laughed. "Yeah, I'll cook, Jax. Show me

what we've got."

I ended up making stir fry and we ate quietly as we listened to the sounds of a storm brewing outside.

Just as Jaxon cleared our plates, his phone rang and he frowned as he answered it. "Hey, Mia. Everything okay? Jesus. Don't touch *anything*. Yeah, I'll be there in a few."

"What's going on?" I asked.

"I need you to stay here," he demanded, grabbing his wallet and keys. "Do not open the door for anyone, keep the blinds pulled, and for God's sake, don't turn your phone on."

I blinked back tears. "You're scaring me, Jaxon. What the hell is going on?"

He stepped over to me standing by the island and slid his hands to my neck. "Someone killed Wendy's cat."

"The stalker?"

"I don't want to jump to conclusions, but I'm also not going to take any chances, so I need you to stay here until I get back."

"What do I do if someone comes here?"

"Don't open the door," he repeated.

I bit my lip. "I don't like this."

He ran his thumb down my cheek. "I won't be long."

"What if there's an emergency? If I can't turn

my phone on, I can't call you."

"If you're really in trouble, turn your phone on and text me, then turn it right back off," he instructed.

I nodded, and Jaxon leaned down to kiss me gently. "I won't be long. Lock up behind me."

"Okay," I said, and he left me.

SEVEN

Jaxon

I DROVE THE ATV back to Patrick and Wendy's, parking it back in the workshop, then heading to the house. I let myself in the back, and called out, "Anyone home?"

"In the kitchen," Mia called.

"You still here alone?" I asked, a little irritated that she'd left the back door unlocked.

"Yeah, why?"

"Back door was unlocked."

"No it wasn't," she countered, crossing her arms. "Shit. Do you think…?"

"Where did you find Pumpkin?"

She shuddered. "Front porch."

"Did the cameras pick anything up?"

"Only someone in a hoodie dropping her body there."

"Nothing from the back?" I asked.

Mia rubbed her arms and shook her head. "No."

"Did you lock it after we left?" I asked.

She bit her lip and sighed. "It's possible I didn't."

"Well, it's locked now. I'm going to go and take some pictures and see what I can figure out."

"Okay, bud, thanks."

I headed out onto the front porch and called Brock. "Hey."

"Hey," I said. "The Dennis's cat was mutilated. Decapitated."

"Shit, seriously?"

"Yeah, right after the paparazzi showed up at their house, a tip off that Melody was here." I scanned the area, but saw nothing.

"Jesus. Well, she's not there. I'm lookin' right at her," Brock said.

"I know." I turned back to the evidence at

hand. "Harmony's pretty sure Melody's the one who called in the 'tip' just to mess with her."

"Sister revenge is brutal."

"Yep," I said. "I sent you evidence pics. I have no idea where the head is, but if I find it, I'll gather what I can from that as well."

"Okay," he said. "Did you send them to Dallas as well?"

"Yeah. And Matt."

"Okay. We'll work it from this end. Let Harmony know her sister's safe."

"I will. Thanks, brother."

"Sure."

We hung up and I let myself back in the house. "Mia?"

"Still here," she called from the kitchen.

I made my way there, and found her scooping ice cream into a cone. I leaned across the island and smiled.

"Want some?" she asked.

I shook my head. "Nah, I'm good. I don't like the idea of leaving you here alone."

"Mom and Dad'll be home in like, five minutes."

"I'll hang out for a bit, then."

"Knock yourself out," she said, throwing the ice cream back in the freezer drawer, then grabbing a glass of wine. "I'm gonna eat and drink my feelings."

I chuckled. "Sounds like a plan."

Just as I sat on the sofa, the front door beeped and Wendy called out, "Harmony?"

"Nope. Just me, Mom," Mia called back.

"And me," I said.

"Mia? What are you doing here, honey?" Wendy asked, dropping her purse on the kitchen peninsula. "What happened to Seattle?"

"Long story. I think you should sit down, though."

"Why?" she asked, sitting down slowly.

"Someone kind of murdered your cat."

Wendy gasped. "What?"

"Jesus, Mia," I hissed.

"It's the wine," she said. "Sorry, Mom. I didn't mean to just blurt that out."

Wendy shook her head, tears running down her face. "I raised you, honey, I know you. But this sucks."

"We're going to figure out who did it," I promised.

"What happened?" she asked.

"I don't think you want the gory details," Mia said.

"That bad?"

"Like, no head bad."

"Jesus Christ," I muttered.

I adored Mia. She was cool as fuck, but she'd never had a filter and that often got her into trouble. She was not the person you looked to for comfort in a difficult situation for that very reason. But if you wanted the truth, and wanted it from someone who truly cared about you, she was your woman.

Mia let out a frustrated squeak. "Sorry, Mom. Seriously, I'm two glasses into this bottle."

"It's okay, honey. I think I might join you." She headed to the kitchen and returned with a wine glass, and poured wine into it. "The only good thing about this situation is that Pumpkin was really old and had been diagnosed with cancer. She didn't have very long to live anyway. Where's Harmony?"

"With the recent developments, I think it's best I keep Harmony somewhere close to me," I said.

"I'm so sorry we couldn't keep her safe, honey," Wendy said.

"Don't say that, Wendy," I countered. "You've been amazing. I'm more concerned about you guys getting caught in the fray, so if I keep Harmony isolated a bit, I can protect everyone."

"Well, you are both welcome anytime."

"Thank you. I will get your key back to you

tomorrow."

"No rush, honey."

I rose to my feet. "I should get back."

"Don't be a stranger," Mia said.

I chuckled. "Hey, Pot, I'm Kettle."

"Touché."

"Call me next time you're in Portland, okay?" I said. "I bet Cass misses you as well."

"I'll do that," she promised.

"Lock up behind me, okay?"

Wendy nodded and followed me to the door, hugging me, then locking the door as I headed to my truck.

I spent ten minutes driving through our little town in case anyone was following me, then made my way back to the barn when I was sure I was clear. I parked inside and locked the double doors before climbing the stairs to the apartment and letting myself inside.

"Harmony? It's me."

I heard a quiet squeak, and turned the light on just as Harmony peeked out from the hall closet, a baseball bat in her hand. "You scared me to death."

I grimaced. "Sorry."

She set the bat back into the closet and closed the door, nodding toward me. "What's that?"

"Guitar."

She closed the distance between us. "You ran home to get it?"

"No, it was in my truck, so I figured you owed me a song."

"Okay." She smiled. "How did it go?"

"Fine. I've sent all the evidence photos to my team. We're going to hole up here for a little while."

"Please tell me you have movies or something to fill the time with. I mean, I'm all for a sing-along, but maybe tomorrow and the television doesn't seem to have cable. There weren't even rabbit ears to mess with," she said. "I'll go nuts if I'm stuck in here with nothing to do."

"Oh, I have several ideas of things we can do."

"*With* our clothes on," she countered.

"Damn." I chuckled. "I will figure something out."

"Do you see now that it's Melody in danger, not me?"

"Nope," I said.

"You're not a very good FBI person, FYI."

"You don't think?" I asked, heading to the kitchen for a beer.

"You can't see the evidence right in front of you."

I smiled. "I'm a big enough man to admit

when I'm wrong, Rufus, but in this case, I'm confident I'll be proven right."

"Rufus?"

"I was hoping if I used the naked mole rat's name, it would encourage you to get naked."

She rolled her eyes. "I'm not opposed to the idea, but I'd like more wine and the chance to get my heartbeat back to normal."

I frowned. "You still freaked?"

"A little bit, yes."

Setting my beer on the counter, I stepped around the island and pulled her into my arms. She slid her arms around my waist and leaned heavily against me.

* * *

Harmony

I knew I'd been scared, but I didn't realize the extent of it until I was against his body and in the safety of his beefy arms. "Who is doing this?"

"I don't know, but we're going to find out, Harmony. I promise."

"I just don't understand people, you know?" I continued. "We've met some of the nicest people on the planet, but on the flipside of that are some of the worst. I just don't get it."

"I hear you," he said, giving me a gentle squeeze.

"I think I'm just going to go home when all of this is over and maybe set myself up in a little beach house on Tybee Island."

"That sounds perfect," he whispered.

"I'll probably dye my hair…maybe red, I've always liked red, so no one will recognize me," I rambled.

"Don't do that, baby. How will I find you in a crowd?"

"There won't be any crowds. I'll be alone." I squeezed my eyes shut, forcing back tears. "This will all be over, Jaxon. You'll go back to your life and I'll go back to mine."

He lifted my chin and kissed me gently. "Let's make a deal. No talking about going back to our lives, separately, until we have to do that, okay? I'd like to pretend we're in a little happy bubble for a few days."

I stared up at him through watery eyes. "Are you always this much of a bleeding heart?"

He grinned. "Pretty much."

"I kind of like it," I admitted.

"Good. Just don't tell anyone. I've worked to maintain a standoffish image."

"Secret's safe with me," I said.

He kissed me quickly and headed back to the kitchen. "You promised to sing for me, so that's gonna happen tomorrow."

"We agreed on a duet situation, here," I reminded him. "Deal breaker for me, buddy."

"Okay, Rufus, but not until tomorrow," he said, handing me a glass of wine.

I smiled and took a long sip.

* * *

I sat up with a start, a little disoriented and unclear as to where I was. Then I remembered. I'd gone to bed alone. Because I'd said I wanted to go to bed alone. But now, I was sitting in the dark, my heart racing, and I no longer wanted to be alone.

I tiptoed out of the bedroom and down the short hall into the living room. Jaxon was sound asleep on the sofa, the blanket at his waist, his bare chest on display and I seriously wanted to lick every inch of it.

He shifted and I suddenly found his eyes on me. "You okay?" I shook my head and he sat up. "What's wrong?"

I bit my lip. "Bad dream."

Pushing the blankets off, he stood, and made his way to me. "Come on."

He took my hand and led me back to bed, climbing in beside me, and pulling me close. I slid my hand across his stomach and snuggled close.

"Do you remember your dream?" he asked.

"No. Just the terror."

"I hate that," he said, scrubbing a hand down his face.

"I'm sorry I shut you out."

"Don't be sorry."

"Well, it's hard for me not to be."

He ran his fingers up my back. "Yeah?"

"Can I confess something? Partly because I'm punch drunk tired, but mostly because I trust you more than anyone I've ever known?"

He chuckled. "Yeah, baby, confess away."

"I guess I already confessed it. I feel like we've had twenty-five years of trust built up in a matter of days. Is that weird?"

"Yes, I guess in theory. But I feel the same way about you."

"Is this transference?" I asked.

Jaxon chuckled. "Possibly." He rolled me so he hovered over me and stroked my cheek. "You willing to stick around for a bit once all this shit's over and get to know me in a real world setting?"

"Yes."

He grinned, leaning down to kiss me and I slid my hands under the waistband of his boxer briefs, pushing them off. He slid my tank top up and over my tits, drawing a nipple into his mouth and biting down gently. I mewed as the sensation zipped all the way to my clit.

He kissed his way down my belly, tugging my panties off and covering my mound with his mouth. I wove my fingers into his hair and gripped his scalp as his tongue dipped into my pussy and then ran between my folds and to my clit.

"Fuck," he breathed out and I heard the tearing of foil, then he was inside of me and all was right with the world.

He kissed me as he dragged my hands above my head and kept them anchored to the bed as he buried himself inside of me over and over again. I wrapped my legs around his waist, unable to do anything else as he fucked me senseless. I cried out his name as a climax washed over me, and he covered my mouth with his as his dick pulsed inside of me.

"You're so fucking beautiful, Harmony," he whispered, kissing me again, then he took care of the condom and pulled me over his chest.

"I love sex with you," I whispered, kissing his chest.

He smiled. "Ditto."

"Can I ask you a personal question?" I whispered.

"Yep."

"How many people have you slept with?"

"Not a fan of bringing past partners into bed,

Harmony," he said. "I'll answer your question, but tomorrow and somewhere else."

"Oh, okay."

"I'm gonna ask you the same thing, Rufus."

I sighed. "Mine's easy. There were two."

"If I don't want to talk about my past in this bed, I sure as hell don't want to talk about yours."

I bit back a smile. "Well, I just wanted you to know. Only two. Neither of which were any good."

"We can drill down on that tomorrow."

"I'd like you to drill down on me tonight, if you don't mind."

"I can do that," he said with a chuckle. "On your knees."

"Seriously?"

"Yeah, baby, gonna show you something amazing."

I rolled over and sat up on my knees. Jaxon knelt behind me, kissed my shoulder, and guided me onto my hands, then I heard the tear of foil and he was entering me from behind. Oh, my god, it was amazing indeed.

"You okay?" he asked, kissing the rise of my ass and sliding deeper.

"God, yes." I dropped my head back and pressed my butt against him. "Harder."

"Jesus," he hissed and gripped my hips,

slamming into me faster and faster.

"Jax!" I screamed. "Now!"

My body shook as an orgasm covered me and Jaxon fell with me onto the mattress, spooning me and continuing to thrust into me. He built me up again and I slid my hand between my legs, unable to stop myself.

"Yeah, baby, that's right. Touch yourself," he prodded and I moved my finger faster and faster, matching the rhythm of his hips, arching my back as another orgasm slammed into me.

I felt his dick pulse as his arms wrapped around me and he kissed my shoulder. "Jesus, that was hot."

"Seriously," I agreed, still trying to catch my breath. "You're going to ruin me for anyone else, you realize that."

"That's my plan," he retorted, and a thrill hit my heart, followed by a stab of fear. "Whoa," he said. "What just happened?"

"Nothing," I lied, breaking our connection and rushing to the bathroom. I closed the door and locked it, flipping on the shower so he wouldn't hear me cry.

"Rufus," Jaxon said, from right behind me.

I let out a quiet squeak as I spun to face him. He frowned. "Shit, why are you crying?"

"Because I'm a girl."

His eyes got soft and he smiled gently, sliding his hand to my neck. "Hey. Why are you crying?"

"I don't know, honestly. I just felt like this was all going to go to shit and it freaked me out."

"Why do you think it's gonna go to shit?"

"Because I'm Harmony Morgan and that's how it goes in my world."

He stroked my cheek and kissed me quickly. "Not anymore, it doesn't."

"I think you're underestimating the power of the Harmony Morgan world. It's formidable."

He chuckled, lifting me into the shower, then stepping in himself. "Didn't you know that in the Jaxon Quinn world, you're always protected?"

"Yes, but I'm just visiting your world, so it won't last long."

"Okay, we're gonna stop all definitive statements until all this shit's dealt with, hear?" he said. "I like where we're at, and I plan to stay here as long as I can. Are you with me?"

I bit my lip, then nodded. "What the hell. Let's throw caution to the wind."

He laughed and kissed me, then guided me under the water. I dipped my head back, closing my eyes and letting the spray wash away my doubts. At least for the moment.

Jaxon

HARMONY AND I stayed in our love bubble for two days and then it was time to get back to the real world and to say I was a little nervous about that was an understatement. She and I had spent hours singing and generally messing around musically, and even managed to write a song together. She was talented and gorgeous, and I wanted more.

We were currently heading back to Portland; Brock and Dallas confident they'd identified the stalker and had him locked up where he couldn't touch the Morgan sisters for the moment.

I was still restless, though. Harmony didn't recognize Joey Walters, the young kid found lurking outside the hotel suite, and there was never any surveillance of him anywhere near the hotel until last night. He swore he was innocent, which every suspect did, but in this case, I was leaning toward believing him and I couldn't put my finger on why.

This gorgeous woman sitting next to me was under my skin in a beautiful way, but the closer we got to 'home,' the more she retreated. Both physically and emotionally. I reached over and took her hand again, and she held it, but just for a few minutes before pulling away and staring out the window.

I didn't push. I left her alone with her thoughts but I wasn't going to leave her there for long. I was falling for her, hard.

Instead of taking her back to the hotel, I pulled up to my home in North Portland. Harmony glanced at me, then back out the window. "Where are we?"

"My place."

"You mean, your home?"

"Yes," I said.

"Why?"

"Because I figured you might need a day before jumping back into the mess."

"Really?" She looked at me with watery eyes. Damn, she was cute. Not a lick of makeup meant her freckles were on display, and her hair was piled on top of her head in a messy bun with a few tendrils falling down her cheeks.

I frowned. "Unless you want to go back to the hotel?"

She shook her head. "No. I really, really don't."

I grinned. "Okay, then come inside and we'll figure out a game plan going forward."

She climbed out of my truck faster than I could, and leaned back inside. "Hurry up, slowpoke. I want to see how the great Jaxon Quinn lives."

Her joy was contagious and I slid out of the driver's seat and led her to the front door, stepping back so she could precede me inside, grateful my cleaning lady had come yesterday.

* * *

Harmony

I walked into the foyer and smiled. His home was clean, in fact, it was newly cleaned, and although it was sparse furniture-wise, it was really nice. The foyer opened up to a spacious living room, a granite peninsula separating the room from the semi-galley kitchen, and a small round dining room table sat in front of a bay window overlooking an atrium of sorts.

"Wow, Jax, this is really cute."

He grinned, closing and locking the door behind him after he reset the alarm. "Yeah?"

"Whoever decorated did a really good job."

"Cassidy helped out a bit, but it was mostly me." He cocked his head. "Actually, if you like it, it was her. If you don't, it was me."

I chuckled. "Cassidy's married to…?"

"Carter. Ace."

"Right. I will never remember that," I admitted.

"Once you meet them, you'll remember."

"I get to meet them?"

"Yeah, this is day one of us getting to know each other in the real world."

I turned away from him and bit back tears. God, I wish I could believe that.

"Nope," he said, and took my hand, spinning me to face him again. "We're not doing that."

"Jax," I said with a sigh.

"Lean in, Rufus, we're doing this."

"I'm not good at leaning in."

"No shit?" he deadpanned.

I rolled my eyes.

"How about you just relax and let me do the figurin'?"

I looped my arms around his neck. "Okay, Gazzo."

"Shit, you know Gazzo?"

"I happen to love the entire Rocky franchise."

"See? I knew you were perfect," he said, leaning down to kiss me.

I broke the kiss and stroked his cheek. "You really want me to be all in?"

"Yeah."

"I'm not always in this good of a mood. Sometimes I'm difficult."

He grinned. "I already figured that out."

"You just lost points, buddy. You're supposed to tell me I'm never difficult."

"If you really were never difficult, then you'd never be any fun, and I didn't sign up for boring."

I raised an eyebrow. "Oh, *really*? You signed up?"

"Sure did."

"How come I didn't get the chance to do that?"

He raised an eyebrow. "Because you're not always in a good mood and difficult."

I burst out laughing, dropping my head to his

chest. "Oh, my god."

He gave me a gentle squeeze and kissed me again. "You hungry?"

"Starving."

"Let me see what's in my fridge. We might need to go out."

"Or we can run to the store and I can cook."

He grinned. "Yeah, baby, I'm all over you cooking."

"You're ridiculously easy to please."

"Am I?"

"It certainly seems that way, but it could also be good timing." I nodded. "I love to cook and never get the chance, so it's a win-win."

"I'll check the fridge and see what we need," he said. "Make yourself at home."

I took a little stroll through his house, peeking into rooms and 'making myself at home.' He had three bedrooms, one filled with gym equipment, and having investigated every inch of his body, I was fairly confident he used all of it. The other spare bedroom was filled with some of the most gorgeous guitars I'd ever seen. This was obviously where he made music, because there was a drum set against the wall with the window, a desk in the corner with a laptop on it, and microphone stands scattered in various places, some with mics on them, some without. There was a gorgeous upright piano in front of the window and I couldn't help but sit down and play a little before snooping further.

I walked back into the hall and found a bathroom and a laundry room across from the bedrooms, then made my way to the master at the end of the hall. I walked into the room and smiled. It was so, I don't know, very much him. The headboard of the bed looked like it was made out of reclaimed wood, but the bedding looked super chic. White on white with pops of blue, so I could only assume this was Cassidy's doing. I could see a bathroom and closet on the west wall, and a huge window that overlooked tall trees, which provided privacy and something pretty to look at.

"You like?"

I jumped in fright, spinning to find Jaxon leaning against the doorframe, his arms crossed, and looking edible.

"I love," I said. "It's very you."

"Did I hear you playing my piano?"

I chuckled. "Guilty."

"I can't wait to hear more." He closed the distance between us. "I like you in my space, Harmony."

"You do?"

"Very much." He smiled, settling his hands

on my hips. "I'd actually like to see you naked in my space."

I raised an eyebrow. "What about the store?"

"I've got everything we need. We don't need to go to the store."

I twirled my finger toward him. "Strip."

"I'm sorry?"

"You heard me. Strip. Slowly."

His mouth twitched and he pulled his T-shirt over his head. Good lord, his chest should be deemed illegal. I bit my lip and forced myself not to help him.

"Slower," I directed as his hands went to the waistband of his jeans.

He slid his jeans down his legs and threw them in the corner. He was barefoot which was sexy as hell, and I could see the evidence of his arousal under his boxer briefs.

"Your turn," he said.

"Are you naked?" I challenged, and he grinned.

"You gotta give me something, Rufus."

I reached under my T-shirt and removed my bra, dropping it on the floor.

"Okay, that's not entirely fair," he complained. "At least take the T-shirt off as well."

I did as he requested, then smiled. "Do not

move," I demanded.

He watched me intently as I closed the distance between us and knelt in front of him, tugging his boxer briefs off and releasing his dick. I wrapped my fingers around his girth and squeezed gently, then licked the tip.

"Jesus," he hissed.

"Do not move," I repeated.

He smiled down at me and stroked my cheek. "I won't move."

I took him in my mouth, sucking the tip, then taking him as deep as I could before choking myself. I slid my hand down the shaft, working it as I continued to suck. God, he tasted incredible and I couldn't get enough. His hands wove into my hair, tugging my locks out of the scrunchy I'd used to secure it to the top of my head, and he gripped my scalp as I sucked and licked my way to heaven.

When his hips started to move, I grabbed his ass and held on while he fucked my face, spurring my arousal on with each thrust.

"I'm gonna come, baby," he warned and I held on tighter. "Harmony."

"Come," I mumbled, my mouth full of his goodness.

"Jesus," he rasped again, and held my head

tighter as he thrust twice more and shuddered with his release. I took every drop and swallowed, running my tongue up the length once more because I wasn't quite ready to stop tasting him.

Without warning, his hands hooked me under my arms and I was dropped on the mattress and the rest of my clothes were removed in record time. Then his mouth was on my core and I was gripping his scalp just to keep my body from floating away.

His mouth moved to my clit and he slid two fingers inside of me, sweeping my walls and hitting that oh so amazing spot deep inside. I cried out as I came and then he was over me and thrusting deep while I arched to get closer.

"Oh, god," I moaned as my body threatened to come undone. "I can't wait, honey."

"Don't wait," he demanded. "Jesus, you feel incredible."

I grabbed his shoulders for support and let myself go, arching again as my body let go. He wasn't far behind, but his angry "Fuck" gave me pause. "What's wrong?"

"Forgot a condom," he snapped. "Shit, baby, I'm sorry."

"It's okay," I said, sitting up on my arms.

"I'm on the pill."

"That's not really the point," he argued, making his way to the bathroom. "I should have been more careful." He returned with a warm washcloth and settled it between my legs. "You just came out of nowhere with that fucking delicious mouth of yours."

"You're the delicious one." I grinned. "Lordy, I could snack on you all day."

Stretching out beside me, he pulled me over his chest and kissed my temple. "I won't forget again, Harmony. I promise. And I'll get bloodwork done this week."

"I trust you. I mean, I'll be pissed if I find crabs in my twat, but I believe you when you say you're clean."

"Fuck me," he groaned, obviously trying to stop a laugh. "There will be no crabs in your twat, Harmony. That I can promise you."

"Isn't twat just the best word? It's so versatile."

He laughed. "Jesus."

"But you have to say it the British way. Twat. Not like we do, twot. You know what I mean?"

His shoulders shook with laughter, but he managed to roll me onto my back and kiss me deeply. "You seriously need to stop saying twot."

"Twat," I corrected "Try again."

He raised his face to the ceiling like he was concentrating, then drew out, "Twaaaat."

"Now you've somehow added a 'w.' What the hell?" I demanded, and he dropped his head to my shoulder, laughing harder. I couldn't stop a grin, slipping my fingers into his hair as he continued to laugh on top of me.

"I think you might be the funniest person I've ever met," he said once he could breathe.

"You *think*?" I challenged. "I was literally put on this earth for comic relief. I *am* the funniest person you've ever met and I would suggest you recognize that fact immediately."

He grinned, leaning down to kiss me. "I apologize. I will never take that for granted again."

I stroked his cheek. "You're a very smart man."

"You gonna cook now?"

"You're hungry, huh?"

"You're a very smart woman."

I laughed and slid off the bed. Once I cleaned up and put on one of his T-shirts, I made my way to the kitchen to see what I could create.

After dinner, Jaxon offered to do the dishes while I soaked in his kickass clawfoot tub, and I didn't object. Lord, I needed this. The hotel had a hot tub, but I hadn't had a proper bath in ages.

"You want some company?" Jaxon asked from the doorway.

I'd been soaking for close to twenty minutes and was debating getting out or adding more hot water.

"Depends on who the company is," I retorted.

He grinned, leaning down to kiss me quickly, just as his doorbell pealed through the house.

"Fuck," he breathed out, sliding his phone out of his jeans pocket. "It's Brock. Raincheck."

I nodded and watched him walk away.

* * *

Jaxon

I pulled open the door and forced a smile. "Hey, brother."

"Hey. Figured you'd want to see what I found," Brock said, and stepped inside.

"You could have called."

He raised an eyebrow. "I could have, you're right. But I—"

"Hi," Harmony said, and I met her eyes. "Sorry, I didn't mean to interrupt, I was just going to grab some water."

Jesus, she looked cute with her hair piled back on top of her head, tight yoga leggings, and an off the shoulder sweatshirt. I wanted to kick

Brock out of my house and peel her out of her clothes.

"No problem," Brock said. "I'm Brock, it's nice to meet you."

"Harmony." She shook his hand. "Nice to meet you, too. I'll get out of your hair."

She grabbed a bottled water, gave me a sweet smile, then headed back to my bedroom.

"So it's like that, huh?" Brock mused.

"Not a fuckin' word," I warned. "Remember, I kept my mouth shut about Bailey."

Brock raised his hands in surrender, but I didn't miss his shit-eating grin. "Message received."

"What did you find?" I grumbled and he spread the files across my kitchen table.

* * *

Harmony

I heard the beep of the alarm about an hour into a rerun of House, and peeked into the hallway. "Jax?"

"All clear," he called and I padded out to the kitchen where papers were strewn about the table.

"Do you recognize this guy?" he asked, pointing to a file.

I leaned over and studied the photo. My

stomach churned and I nodded. "That's Graham. He's Billy's on-again/off-again boyfriend. Why?"

"He's the one who bought the rat, amongst other things. He paid the kid we caught a grand to deliver it."

I frowned. "Why would he do that?"

"We don't know. We haven't been able to find him. Yet."

"What does Billy say?"

"He refuses to believe Graham would do this, but he said if he contacts him, he'll let us know."

"He will," I confirmed. "Billy's our best friend, Jax. He would never betray us, not even for Graham."

"I hope you're right."

"Me too," I admitted. "Does that mean we're staying here for a little longer?"

He smiled gently. "You sound hopeful."

"That's because I am. I love your home, Jaxon. I feel safe."

"I'm glad." He pulled me against him and wrapped his arms around me. "And, yeah, you can stay as long as you want."

"I'm going to need to get a few more things from the hotel. Or go shopping."

"Which would you prefer?"

I sighed. "I should probably check in with

my sisters. Lyric's more than likely worried sick."

"We'll swing by tomorrow."

I dropped my head to his chest. "Sounds good."

"You wanna watch a movie and make out?"

I grinned up at him. "I don't know how long I'll be able to stay awake, but that sounds like a great plan."

"You find the movie and I'll open more wine."

NINE

Harmony

J AXON TOOK MY hand and squeezed it once he'd parked in the hotel parking lot. I grimaced and squeezed back, holding his hand like a talisman as he let me have a few minutes to breathe.

"No matter what Melody says, please do not let me kill her," I begged.

His mouth twitched and he nodded. "She calls you a cunt again, I can't guarantee I won't go for her throat."

I raised an eyebrow. "I'd pay good money to see that fight."

He chuckled, leaning over to kiss me quickly. "Ready?"

"No, but let's go anyway."

We climbed out of the truck and walked up to my room. I was able to slip inside without being seen, packing up a few of the things I couldn't live without, then it was time to face the music so to speak, so I headed down the hall to my sister's room.

Before I raised my hand to knock, Jaxon leaned down and kissed me gently. "You got this."

I nodded and pushed into the room. "Melody?"

"Where the hell have you been?" a very angry Lyric snapped, stalking into the room. "I have been trying to call you for days."

I felt Jaxon's hand settle on my back and I leaned into it.

"Oh," Lyric squeaked, freezing in place and staring up at Jaxon. "Who are you?"

"He's one of the FBI agents trying to figure out who's stalking DiDi," I answered.

"Jaxon Quinn, ma'am," he said with a nod.

"Have you found anything?" she asked—

which came out more like a demand. Hopefully, Jaxon overlooked her tone, because she was one of the nicest people on the planet, but she was a lawyer and could sound curt even when she didn't mean to.

"I'm not at liberty to say," he replied. "But rest-assured *both* your sisters are protected."

Her eyes did a full body scan and then glanced at me. "I see that."

I rolled my eyes and she pulled me in for a hug.

"Good lord, NiNi, I was worried sick," she said.

"Sorry Li. It's been a weird couple of days."

She cupped my face. "Are you okay? Melody mentioned she'd been rather nasty."

"Melody mentioned?" I asked.

"Okay, Billy spilled the beans and Melody didn't deny it," Lyric clarified.

"That sounds more accurate," I grumbled. "It's not worth hashing out again. I just came by to pick up a few things. I'm going to stay with a friend for a few days. Did she tell you I quit?"

"No. She conveniently left that part out."

"Well, I did."

"Honey, that seems rash, don't you think? You can't give up on her."

"I'm not giving up on her. I'm doing this because if I don't, I will murder her," I admitted, craning my head to look at Jaxon. "For the purposes of your law-enforcement ears, you didn't hear that."

A flicker of humor lit his eyes, but his facial expression stayed neutral. "Got it."

I focused back on Lyric. "Honestly, LiLi, it's the only way I can fathom salvaging a relationship with her. I miss my sister. The raging lunatic who has replaced her is not someone I care to know."

She frowned. "If you quit, what will you do?"

I shrugged. "I've been saving everything I make for eight years. I can do whatever I want to do."

"Well, there you are," Melody said in a singsong voice as she breezed into the room. "It's about time you got here."

"I'm not here," I corrected. "I'm picking up a few things and then I'm staying with a friend for a few days."

She nodded toward Jaxon. "Is that the 'friend'?"

"That's the 'none of your business.'"

"Why are you being such a bitch?" she snapped.

I felt Jaxon stiffen at my back and I sighed. "Melody, I will no longer take the abuse you're dishing out. I hope that, in time, you'll see this is the best thing for both of us. I'd like to just go back to being your sister, but I cannot be your assistant and stay sane."

She threw her arms in the air. "Well, what the hell am I going to do in the interim?"

"I'll work on a part-time basis and help find someone even better than me. But not until next week. I'm taking some time off."

She crossed her arms and stomped her foot. "I'm shooting next week."

"Which is why I'm not going to leave you high and dry, DiDi," I said, trying to stay as calm as possible. "But you're just running lines right now, so you don't need me. Billy's always been my back-up and he's fantastic."

"But I don't *want* Billy," she whined.

I shrugged. "Well, that's no longer my problem."

"Please, NiNi, you know I can't do this without you."

"Of course you can," I countered. "You're a brilliant and capable young woman. You can do anything you put your mind to."

"You selfish—"

"I'd highly suggest you stop whatever you

intended to say," Jaxon warned.

"And on that note, I'm going to go ahead and take my leave," I said. "I will see you Monday morning bright and early, Melody."

"Dinner on Saturday night?" Lyric asked.

"We'll see."

She hugged me and I tried not to run out of the room. Jaxon followed me back to my room and the second the door closed behind us, I burst into tears and planted my face in his chest.

"Okay, Rufus, I got you," he said, pulling me close.

"I don't want to hate her, Jaxon, but she makes it so fucking hard not to." I slid my arms around his waist. "I just don't understand how we got here. We used to be so close."

"Sometimes shit just happens," he said. "Her trauma crashes into your trauma and you can't find your way through the mess. You just have to do your best and let the rest of it sort itself out. How your sister acts or reacts to something isn't your responsibility." He lifted my chin and stroked my wet cheeks. "All you can control is you, baby, and I think you're doing a pretty fantastic job. Melody's gotta work her own shit out."

"I know all that logically, but why does it hurt so bad anyway?"

"Because you love your sister," he said with a gentle smile.

"That's true. I don't like her right now, but, yes, I do love her."

"Let's get out of here. I'm going to take you out for dinner. Do you like French food?"

"Oh, my god, I love French food."

"Good answer, Rufus."

He kissed me gently and then we headed downstairs and drove to a little hole-in-the wall French bistro. It was exactly what I needed.

* * *

"I can't get over how much food there was," I said as Jaxon drove us back to his home. "We're going to have leftovers for days."

He smiled. "No, we really won't."

"Right, I forgot how much you can eat."

"Oh, hello Pot, I'm Kettle."

"Okay, I forgot how much *I* can eat," I conceded.

He took my hand and linked his fingers with mine. "You up to stopping at the store? That way we can stay in all weekend."

"You mean, we're not going to hike up Mt. Hood?"

He raised an eyebrow. "Do you *want* to hike up Mt. Hood?"

"Hell, no, I do not. I will never want to do

that, but if it's something you like to do, I'm open to trying things you like to do."

"Jesus, you really are perfect," he said with a chuckle.

"Don't go there, Jax."

"Why not?"

"Because it won't last. I don't want you getting your hopes up. I'm letting you see the best of me right now. It won't be long before I'll be scratching myself and farting in front of you."

"Or, if you have an itch, I'll scratch it."

I wrinkled my nose. "Only if you give me crabs, otherwise, I'll be scratching myself."

He let out a deep belly laugh, squeezing my hand as he did it. "Jesus Christ," he hissed, still laughing.

"I may have had more wine than I thought."

"Maybe you haven't had enough," he said, as we pulled into the Fred Meyer parking lot and found a spot close to the front. "Let's rectify that."

I chuckled. "Is your plan to keep me drunk and horny all weekend?"

"Is that an option?"

"Wine makes me horny as hell, so, yes, it's an option."

He grinned. "Let's get in there, then."

We headed inside and stocked up for our love

weekend.

* * *

"You want ice cream?" Jaxon asked, reaching into the fridge for a beer.

"Hells, yes, I want ice cream."

He grinned and handed me a small pint of butter pecan and a spoon, then opened his beer. "You're not going to join me?" I asked.

"I'd rather eat you," he said, waggling his eyebrows. "You're sweeter."

"I can't imagine how that's possible." I slid the spoon into my mouth and closed my eyes. "Mmmm."

Before I registered what was happening, I was grasped around the waist and pulled onto the sofa and onto Jaxon's lap. It was a miracle I didn't drop the ice cream. Since I was straddling him, I leaned down and kissed him gently, then took another bite.

His hands slid under my T-shirt and cupped my breasts. I'd taken my bra off earlier, so he had full access and he was using it to his advantage. He rolled my nipples into tight peaks and I arched into his touch as I continued to eat the ice cream. Lifting my T-shirt, he slipped his head under it and I giggled as he took a nipple into his mouth and sucked.

"Do *not* make me drop my treat," I warned.

He met my eyes. "I thought *I* was your treat."

"Oh, you are." I dripped a little ice cream on the seam of his lips and ran my tongue across it. "But I have to admit, this is a bonus."

He kissed me again, then pushed my T-shirt up, taking my spoon so he could remove my clothing. I ended up with one arm still in my shirt, not willing to give up my ice cream. He cupped my breasts and kissed both of them before taking one nipple in his mouth, then the other.

I let a little ice cream drop onto one breast and I shivered as his tongue licked the sweetness off my skin.

"Fuck," he breathed out, standing. "Hold on."

I let out a squeak and wrapped my arms around his neck and my legs around his waist as he carried me back to the bedroom.

"I'm gonna drop the ice cream," I warned.

"Don't. I just had the floors redone."

"What if I dump it on you?" I challenged.

"I'm all for you licking it off me, baby, but don't get it on the floor."

I grinned as he set me on my feet and pulled his shirt off, moving to slide my yoga pants down my legs. Still holding my dessert, I stepped out of my clothing and stood before him in just my panties.

As he stepped toward me again, I flicked a spoonful of ice cream on his chest and watched it slide down a few centimeters before catching it with my tongue and licking him clean.

"Okay, that's not gonna work," he said, and took my treat away.

"Hey…wait."

He lifted me and dropped me on the bed, then tugged my panties off and buried his face between my legs. I anchored one foot to the mattress and hooked my other leg over his shoulder arching to get closer.

I wove my fingers into his hair as he sucked and licked me into an incredibly delicious orgasm, and then he was over me and his dick was deep inside of me.

"Yes, Jax, don't stop!" I begged as he buried himself deeper and deeper, harder and faster.

"Jesus," he hissed and then his cock pulsed inside of me and I lost my mind as another orgasm hit me hard.

"Oh, my god," I whispered, sliding my hands in his hair as he rolled us to our sides. "That was amazing."

He chuckled. "Glad to hear it. Gonna get rid of the condom."

He headed into the bathroom and returned

with a washcloth, settling it between my legs.

"You're ruining me, you know," I said as he stretched out beside me again and pulled me against him.

"How so?"

"I will never be satisfied—"

His kiss cut off my sentence. "You won't need to be satisfied by anyone other than me, Harmony, so let's get this straight now."

"We still haven't had 'the talk,'" I pointed out.

He sighed and slid off the bed.

"Where are you going?"

"We're not doing it here," he said, pulling on his boxer briefs. "We'll talk in the living room. Panties only."

I chuckled. "Kinky but okay."

I snagged my panties off the floor and shimmied them on, then followed him out to the living room. He pulled me onto his lap in his over-stuffed recliner. "Six women, none of them were love matches, they all lasted less than six months, except one. She and I were in a 'thing' for almost two years, but she had some ulterior motives, so I cut ties."

"What kind of ulterior motives?"

"She had a brother in jail and thought if she sucked me off enough, I'd hide evidence before his trial."

I wrinkled my nose. "Oh, my god, that's awful. Were you hurt?"

"Honestly? No." He stroked my cheek. "Full disclosure, if you pulled something like that, I'd be hurt, Harmony."

That both surprised me and made me feel all mushy inside. "You would?"

"Yeah, baby, I would."

"Wow," I whispered. "I would never do that to you."

He grinned. "I know."

I licked my lips. "I've had sex with two men...well, three now, but one in high school, it was awful, and then with the last guy I dated. I broke up with him over two years ago. Mostly because I found out he was way into my sister and wanted me to pretend to be her in bed."

"No shit?"

"No shit," I said.

"Did that hurt?"

"Yeah, Jax, it hurt," I admitted. "But not because I loved him. I have always believed myself to be a really good judge of character and he got through. I was more pissed at myself, if that makes sense."

"Yeah, Rufus, that makes sense."

"It's different with you," I said. "I trust you

like I've never trusted anyone and for some reason, that doesn't scare me. It should. But it
doesn't."

"I will never betray you."

I kissed him quickly. "I believe you."

He smiled. "You want more ice cream?"

I shook my head. "I want a popsicle."

"I don't have any popsicles."

I slid my hand under the waistband of his
boxer briefs. "Yes, you do."

He chuckled and carried me back to the bedroom.

TEN

Harmony

M ONDAY MORNING, JAXON drove
me back to the hotel and walked me up
to Melody's room. She was still in bed,
so I roused her and then joined Jaxon in the living
room.

"Brock's with you today," Jaxon said.

"I know." I smiled. "You told me."

He frowned. "Still not happy about it."

"Hmm-mm," I mused distractedly as I
scrolled through today's schedule on my iPad.

"You told me that, too."

"Rufus?"

"Hmm?" I said and added a note to ask Butchy for a rundown of logistics.

"Harmony?"

I glanced up at Jaxon and sighed. "Yes, Jax. I hear everything you're saying. I understand that you don't like that you're not the one watching us. But can you control that?"

"Not really," he conceded.

"Do you trust your friend?"

"Yes."

I smiled, setting my stuff aside and standing. "Then trust that he's got us. We also have Butchy and he's as protective as you are."

He frowned. "Still don't like it."

I chuckled. "I know."

"If you feel weird, on any level, you tell Brock, and then text me."

"No."

"What the fuck?" he snapped.

"I will tell Brock, but I'm not going to text you as well," I said, patting his chest. "You have *work* to do and I'm not going to interrupt you while you're working."

"And I'm telling you you can."

"Thanks, but it's not gonna happen."

He leaned closer, raising an eyebrow. "Are you seriously saying no to me?"

"Yep." I stood on my tiptoes and touched my nose to his. "Get used to it."

His eyes darkened and I smiled, pressing my lips to his.

"Well, shit," Melody sneered. "No wonder you quit. You're getting your girl dick wet."

I squeezed my eyes shut and took a deep breath before facing my sister. "Good morning, Melody. You look well-rested."

"We're late, thanks to you," she said, and I felt Jaxon stiffen behind me.

"I'm not going to dignify that with a response," I said. "And we're not late. Not even close, but we should get going. Butchy's waiting in the hall for us."

"Brock's on his way up," Jaxon said. "I want you to wait until he gets here."

"Did you not hear me?" Melody asked. "We're late."

Jaxon turned his head to face her, and I could tell he was trying not to verbally eviscerate her. "I *did* hear you. But the safety of you and your sisters is my priority, so you'll leave when my team gets here."

Melody rolled her eyes and swished her hair,

stalking back into her room. A knock came at the suite door and Jaxon peeked through the peephole, then pulled open the door. "Hey, brother."

Brock walked in with another man and I realized I was looking at three of the best looking men I'd ever seen.

"Dallas," Jaxon said, and I noticed him relax a little. "Matt released you, huh?"

"Yeah."

"Harmony, this is Dallas. He's part of our team."

I shook Dallas's hand and smiled. "It's nice to meet you."

"Harmony, come with me for a second," Jaxon said, and I followed him into the office off the living room.

Pushing the door closed, he pulled me into his arms and kissed me far too thoroughly for my liking. And I say that because the second he did it, I wanted to strip him naked and keep him tied up to my bed forever. Instead, we both had to go to our respective jobs and kinky, naked sex would have to wait.

"You're evil," I whispered. "Has anyone ever told you that?"

He smiled, kissing me again. "Yep, but not because I riled them up. This way, anyway."

"I don't know how late I'm gonna be to-night," I warned.

"You just let me know when you want me to pick you up."

I grimaced. "I might need to stay here."

"If you do, I'm here with you," Jaxon said.

"So we're continuing this?" I asked.

"Hell, yeah we are." He frowned. "Unless you don't want to."

"That's kind of a tough call," I said. "I feel like my crops have been sufficiently watered. I'm now concerned about oversaturation. And weevils." I waved my hands over my crotch. "You know, in my twat."

"Jesus Christ," he hissed as he dropped his head back and laughed, before kissing me again. "Not gonna lie, I'm gonna miss you."

I wrinkled my nose. "Me too."

He kissed me again and walked me back out to his partners before walking out the door.

* * *

With Butchy leading our little team, and Brock and Dallas following, we piled into two SUVs and headed to the lot. Filming of one of the more raunchy sex scenes was happening today, so it would be a closed set. Not even Butchy would be allowed inside and I wasn't sure how the FBI agents would deal with that.

Only I would be on set with the director, actors, and camera man, and Billy had been bitching all morning about how unfair it was that he, as Melody's hair and makeup, couldn't be there as well.

"It's not like I haven't seen your tits before," he whined. "Multiple times."

"Yeah," Melody agreed.

"It's not just about you, though," I reminded her. "Deacon has to feel comfortable as well."

"Why would he care if Billy's there?" Melody asked.

"I don't think it's any of our business why. He has a right to not have everyone see his junk wrapped up in a little bag," I said.

Butchy snorted from the driver's seat, but didn't comment.

"Sorry, it's not really a *little* bag. I don't want to make it seem like he's lacking," I clarified and Billy let out a girly swoon noise.

"*Girl*, are you seriously telling me that right now? I want in on that set."

"No one's getting on the set, honey," I pressed. "I'd be fine not being there as well, but they made a concession for Melody."

"I'll go instead of you," Billy offered.

"Maybe if you could be trusted not to jack

off in the corner…" Butchy mused.

"Fuck you," Billy ground out, but there wasn't any heat behind it.

I shrugged. "It is what it is, Billy. Sorry."

We arrived at the set, thankfully cutting off more of Billy's whining, and Melody and I waited in the back seat until Dallas and Brock opened our doors.

Butchy was not happy these two men had usurped his duty, which I'd heard all about for the three minutes he and I had been left alone in the SUV before leaving the hotel.

I did my best to assure him that this had nothing to do with him not doing his job. We adored Butchy and had no intention of replacing him. The agents needed to find the stalker and that meant Butchy could do what we needed him to do…guard us. He'd seemed placated for the moment, but I wasn't sure how long that would last.

He pressed his lips together and climbed out of the front seat, Billy following, and stood off to the side observing everything as Dallas and Brock flanked me and Melody. We headed inside and our day started with Billy raiding the crafts services table.

He was apparently over being left off the set.

Once they'd loaded their plates, Melody and

Billy took off for wardrobe and I grabbed a muffin and coffee before the craziness started.

* * *

"Shit!" Deacon hissed, and I looked up from my iPad, immediately wishing I hadn't.

"You okay?" Melody asked, leaning up on her elbows, and grinning at him with a knowing smile.

I squeezed my eyes shut. Deacon had a rather impressive erection and Melody was apparently enjoying his discomfort.

She, of course, was completely naked and had no issues showing off her body. She had a beautiful body, slim through the waist, nice full B-cupped breasts, and a perfect shaped butt. In contrast, Lyric was smaller in the chest and hip area, whereas I'd gotten what they didn't, in spades. I was a DD on a good day and my butt would never require surgical endowment. I also had a fluctuating waistline, depending on how much ice cream I devoured.

I bit my lip. Thinking about ice cream brought Jaxon to mind and I shivered in anticipation of tonight. I knew beyond a shadow of a doubt that he'd make me feel just like I did yesterday, and the day before, and—

"Harmony!" my sister snapped.

Shaken out of my erotic thoughts, I realized

I'd been chewing the end of my pen, so I set it down and focused on my sister. "Yes, Melody?"

"I need water."

I rolled my eyes. "Let me get on that right away, oh exalted one."

I walked to the table at the back of the room, snagged a water off it, and took it to my sister. I tried my best to avert my gaze, seriously not wanting to see any more of either of them. I'd had enough boobs and family jewels to last a lifetime.

No, that wasn't entirely true. I was all about Jaxon's family jewels, and I didn't have a problem with my boobs, but other people's pink bits could stay firmly behind fabric.

"Ready to try that again?" Jay asked, and Deacon nodded.

I focused back on my iPad as the exaggerated groaning and skin slapping against one another continued.

By the time Jay called, "Cut!" I was keyed up and feeling claustrophobic. We'd been stuck in this room for five hours, and that was after a short lunch, without a break and I was done. I wanted wine and my man.

And not necessarily in that order.

"Good job, everyone," Jay said. "We'll see you back tomorrow morning, six a.m."

Tomorrow would begin the final of the three longest sex scenes. More pink bits. Joy. I checked my watch. It was seven p.m. Damn, it was gonna be a long week.

We filed out of the studio and I took my phone out of the locked box everyone was forced to drop their internet devices into. I noticed I had six missed texts and two missed phone calls from Jaxon and realized I hadn't warned him I'd be incommunicado.

I dialed his number just as movement caught my attention from my peripheral vision and I glanced up to see him walking toward me. I let out a quiet squeak and made a run for him. "You're here?"

He caught me and held me close. "Yeah, Rufus, I'm here."

"I'm so sorry I didn't call you back. I had to lock my phone up during shooting."

"I know. I called Brock."

I met his eyes. "You did?"

"Yeah. Was freakin' out a little when my second call went unanswered, so I called him and he filled me in."

I relaxed. "Are you sure *you're* not the stalker?"

Jaxon smiled. "Maybe not say that so loud."

I grimaced. "Good point."

"You ready to go?"

"With you?"

"Yep. Dallas is with your sister tonight."

"Oh, my god, really?" I asked hopefully. "I don't have to go back to the hotel? I get you all night?"

He chuckled. "Yeah, Rufus, I'm all yours."

I bit my lip. "Good. 'Cause, I got plans."

"Well, come on," he said, and we made our way out to his car.

ELEVEN

Harmony

"YES!" I HISSED as Jaxon slammed into me from behind. I'd insisted he take me home and fuck me before dinner, because I'd been fantasizing about him all day and I needed relief.

We started off in a reverse cowgirl position, but I was now on all fours, my ass to the air as he penetrated deep and I screamed as I came for the third time.

He wasn't far behind and held my hips as his dick pulsed inside of me. He guided me to the mattress before taking care of the condom and stretching out beside me.

Pulling me onto his chest, he kissed me gently. "How are the weevils?"

"This twat is a very happy twat, thank you very much. The weevils have yet to invade."

He laughed. "I'm glad I can be your own personal pest control."

"I really needed this, Jax." I kissed his chest. "Thank you."

He smiled, stroking my cheek. "You're welcome."

"Did you get everything done today you needed to?"

"Yep. I even had time to run by the clinic and get tested."

"Oh, really?" I settled my chin on his chest and met his eyes. "So, we're taking this to the next level, then."

He raised an eyebrow. "Is that what we're calling it?"

"Leveling up?"

"Will that finally make me a level forty-seven wizard?"

"I'm not sure if you'll be that powerful, I'm

sorry."

"But higher than a level seven house elf, right? I hope?"

I burst out laughing. "Oh, my god, I love you," I said between laughs, and then gasped. "No. I mean—"

He kissed me, cutting me off. "Don't take it back."

"What?"

"Don't take it back." He rolled me onto my back and hovered over me.

"It was a slip of the tongue," I explained.

"Say it for real."

I raised an eyebrow. "You say it first."

He smiled slowly. "I love you."

"Shut up," I said with a snort. "No you don't."

"Yeah, I do."

"You do not."

"Say it," he pressed.

"I want to mean it."

"You *do* mean it," he said.

"I do?"

He kissed me gently. "Yeah, baby, you mean it. You just gotta trust me enough to say it."

"Why are you saying it so soon?"

"Because I feel it."

"Feelings shouldn't always be trusted."

He ran his thumb over my lower lip. "I always trust mine."

"You do?"

He nodded, kissing me again. "It's why I'm good at my job."

"This was just supposed to be a short farming exercise," I grumbled.

"Jesus Christ," he bit out on a laugh. "This."

"This?"

"This is the reason I fell in love with you."

"Because I'm interested in farming?"

"Yes," he deadpanned.

"Jax, this is too fast."

"Who says?"

"Oh, I don't know...common sense?"

He grinned again. "Fuck common sense. I love you. But more importantly, I like you. You make me feel like I've found home."

"Oh, my god, stop being so sweet."

"I'm gonna give you some time to mull this over. You hungry? I'm hungry. I vote finding somewhere in the Pearl tonight." He slid off the bed and headed toward the bathroom.

I heard the water start and followed him. "I can't say it now, you'll just think I'm saying it because I don't want to look like an idiot."

"You know what I'll think? Neat trick," he challenged, stepping into the shower, holding his hand out. "Are you joining me?"

I took his hand and he guided me under the water. "I want to say it, for real, when I'm sure."

He smiled. "Okay."

"Okay?"

"Yeah. Okay."

"Are you mad?"

He cupped my face as I blinked up at him. "Why would I be mad?" he asked.

"Because I need more time."

"I will never be mad at you for needing time, Rufus."

"I just don't want you to think I don't care about you."

"I don't." He kissed me quickly, then poured shampoo into his palm and began to massage it into my scalp.

"You are so uncomplicated," I said, leaning into his hands.

He chuckled. "When you meet my brothers, will you please repeat that? Make sure they're all together, otherwise, you'll need to tell them each individually. In my presence."

"What about my plans to go home?"

"You can go home," he said.

I raised an eyebrow. "I can?"

"Yep. But not without me."

"You have a job."

"I do, you're right. But I also have a shit ton of personal days I haven't used." He guided my head under the water and I closed my eyes as he rinsed my hair. "I'd love to see where you live. Meet your people."

"I don't really have any people anymore. I've been gone for too long. I have a room in Lyric's house where I keep my stuff, but those are my only ties."

"Then why do you need to go home?"

I wiped the water out of my eyes and sighed. "Honestly? I don't know. I guess I just always thought I would."

"What do you have there? A house?" he asked, stroking conditioner through my hair. "Pets? Friends?"

I shook my head. "Just Lyric. And that's huge, but she's got a busy life and I'd probably never get to see her anyway."

"You don't have friends there?"

"When your sister becomes one of the richest children in the world, you soon figure out who your real friends are. I found out quickly I had none. The three of us kind of turned inward and clung to each other." I bit my lip. "God, that sounds so sad."

"No it doesn't. It sounds smart."

"You think?"

"Yeah." He smiled. "If you didn't protect yourself from the jackals, baby, who would?"

"You," I pointed out.

"Well, yeah, *now*." He guided me back under the water and rinsed the conditioner out of my hair. Before I opened my eyes again, his mouth covered mine and he kissed me gently.

"What was that for?" I asked, smiling against his lips.

"Just a reminder I got your back."

I flattened my palms on his pecs and nodded. "I know. I won't ever take that for granted."

He grinned. "I know."

"I love you."

"I know that too."

I rolled my eyes. "I take it back."

"No you don't."

"Yes I do."

"No takebacks times one million," he retorted, stepping under the water and washing his hair.

When his eyes were closed, I knelt in front of him ran my tongue up the underside of his cock.

"Fuck, baby," he growled. "Warn me next time."

"That's not as much fun."

"I take it you're not hungry?"

I sucked the tip of his dick gently. "Let me

do this and then we can eat."

"Twist my arm."

I enjoyed my appetizer and then we got dressed and headed down to the Pearl where we walked and talked and laughed, hitting a couple of bars on the way and enjoying the amazing food Portland had to offer.

* * *

My alarm sounded at five and I groaned as I rolled over and reached for Jaxon. He wasn't in bed, so I sat up and slid my legs over the side of the mattress.

Lordy, I was tired. We'd gotten home just after ten, but I'd been wired and stayed up way later than I should have. Jaxon had taken me to bed at about eleven, but I'd kept him awake with my 'sex shenanigans.' His words.

I honestly didn't know how I was going to get through today. On top of filming, I had interviews to replace me, and I just wanted it done. I was never good with loose ends and as soon as I hired a new assistant for Melody, I planned to get my life settled and exactly where I wanted it to be. I'd never sat down and thought about what I wanted my future to look like, but now that I'd been given permission in a way, I couldn't wait to make plans.

"You're up," Jaxon said as he walked into

the room.

Still sitting on the edge of the bed, I grumbled, "No I'm not. It's an illusion."

He walked toward me, setting a mug on the nightstand. "Your caffeine, m'lady."

"Oh, my god, I love you," I breathed out and took a sip.

"Out the door in thirty, baby."

"Why the hell are you so chipper this morning?"

"Am I?" He chuckled. "I've been up for an hour."

"Why?"

"I don't sleep much."

"I take it back. I hate you."

He grinned, kissing me quickly. "I'm with you today, so you can sleep on the way to the lot."

"Okay," I said, and sighed. "I won't be long."

I took a quick shower and dressed in jeans and a hoodie, piling my hair on top of my head. I didn't give two shits about makeup, I was way too tired, so I didn't bother with it and shuffled to the car where Jaxon let me sleep all the way to the lot.

It wasn't long enough.

"We're here, Rufus," he whispered, kissing me gently.

I forced my eyes open to find him standing in my doorway. "I don't wanna," I whined.

He grinned and squeezed my knee. "We'll get you more coffee inside."

I nodded and climbed out of the car, grabbing my bag and following him inside.

Melody was late, but there was nothing I could do about it, so I set myself up in a corner of the open space and Jaxon found some privacy screens to create a makeshift office.

My first interview arrived twenty minutes later, and then it was game on for three hours straight. I had twenty-five qualified candidates, and twenty-three of them arrived and fangirled for way too long, so they were immediately disqualified. The last thing my sister needed was someone who'd be so starstruck, they wouldn't get anything done. I spent fifteen minutes with them, then cut them loose. There was one girl who couldn't stop talking about Jaxon and how hot he was, so she got cut loose in less time. She was lucky I didn't draw blood as she walked away.

I spent a little more time with the two who didn't fangirl, or ogle my man. Both were highly qualified and no nonsense.

I was currently finishing up with Renee, thankfully my last interview of the day, when my sister came storming into the space. "They put mayo on my sandwich, Harmony. Mayonnaise."

I forced myself not to roll my eyes. "Melody, this is Renee Welsh, she's interviewing for your assistant position."

"Nice to meet you," she said without looking at her, and shoved the sandwich toward me. "Mayo."

"Did you ask them to make you another one? Or, God forbid, make one yourself?" I asked.

"They're out of the good bread."

"Did they put the mayo on both sides?" Renee asked.

"Well, no," Melody confirmed.

"I have an idea." She reached for the plate. "May I?"

"Knock yourself out," I said.

She led Melody around the privacy screen and I watched as they headed to the craft services table.

"Everything okay?" Jaxon asked, stepping over to me.

"We'll see shortly," I said, watching Renee and Melody.

Renee appeared to make Melody a sandwich and my sister took a bite, smiled, then walked away…without throwing a fit.

"She's hired," I said, and Jaxon chuckled. "I'm not joking. She's hired. If she can deal with Melody without killing her, she's a miracle worker."

"You're worried about *Renee* not killing Melody?"

"Yes. I'm not a monster. I still love my sister, even if she's a pain in the ass."

"You're not worried about Melody killing Renee?" he asked.

"Little known fact about my sister. She yells a lot, but she's a chicken shit."

Jaxon nodded. "Thanks for the info."

"Hire her!" Melody yelled across the room.

I gave her a thumbs-up and smiled at Jaxon. "One step closer to freedom."

He grinned and I went about sending all of Renee's information to Lyric so she could run a background check. If all went well, and Renee accepted the terms of the employment offer, I could start my life. Finally.

Renee returned and indicated she'd be interested in the position, so with a promise to be in touch, she went on her way and I gathered all my crap, so I could get the hell out of there.

"You ready?" Jaxon asked.

I nodded. "Who's with my sisters?"

"Matt."

"Your brother?"

"Yes."

I raised an eyebrow. "Do I get to meet him?"

"Do you want to?" he asked.

"Definitely."

His eyes got soft and he smiled. "I love that, Rufus."

"You do?"

He nodded, pulling me behind the screen and kissing me gently. "Love you," he whispered.

"Love you, too."

"We'll head to the hotel after dinner."

"Okay, but I want to change and put on a little makeup if that's okay."

"Why? You look gorgeous."

"Flattery will get you everywhere, even if you're lying."

"I never lie, Rufus."

I rolled my eyes. "Thank you for being sweet, but I'm not meeting your brother in leggings and a hoodie."

"How about we head home, then we can eat at the restaurant in the hotel?"

"That's great. I love that place."

"Me too. Let's head out."

"I'll just check in with my sisters first, okay?"

"Sure." He kissed me quickly, then followed me to where Lyric and Melody were talking with Jay.

* * *

Jaxon

My phone buzzed in my pocket just as I sat down to pull on my boots. Harmony had promised she'd be ready in ten minutes…forty minutes ago. I looked at my screen and frowned. It was Matt. "Hey, big brother. Everything okay?"

"Yeah. Melody's decided she wants everyone at dinner as a group."

"I'm sorry?"

He sighed. "She's booked the restaurant for the entire evening and demanded that you and Harmony, along with all of us—"

"All of us, who?"

"Carter, Aidan, their women. She tried for Luke and Josh as well, but they're not in town. Mack and Darien are on their way."

"Jesus Christ," I hissed.

"He's not gonna save us, brother. She's paying for everything, so we can go for an hour and then get the hell out. Well, you can. I'm with her all night."

"Sorry, not sorry," I grumbled.

Matt laughed. This was classic Matt. Nothing fazed the man. Ever.

"Okay, we'll see you in an hour," I said.

"See you then."

We hung up and I decided to check on Harmony before I put my boots on. She was on her phone pacing my bedroom. "What do you mean she's rented out the entire restaurant?" she snarled. "Oh, my god, LiLi, she's out of control. You're supposed to stop her when she decides to spend two-hundred-grand on dinner!"

I leaned against the doorframe and watched her rage. It was glorious.

"You're joking." She dropped her head back and closed her eyes. "Fine. Yep. Find her Xanax, please, I'm gonna need one...or twelve. Okay, bye."

"You're not really gonna take something not prescribed to you in my presence are you?" I challenged.

"No?"

I chuckled. "Come here."

She walked into my arms and sighed. "I take it you got the message?"

"Matt called." I stroked her back. "Is she really spending that much on dinner?"

"Yep. Apparently, she's been so good with

her discretionary spending that she has it in her entertainment budget Lyric set up for her." She sighed. "But she knows how I feel about crowds."

I lifted her chin and smiled. "I promise you're gonna be fine. These are my people and they're all great."

"Well, if they're anything like you, of course they are."

I kissed her quickly. "You look beautiful."

"Thanks."

"Are you ready?"

She wrinkled her nose, and she was so fucking cute, all I wanted to do was peel off her clothes and keep her in bed all night. "No. I mean, technically, yes, but emotionally, not really."

"I got you, Rufus," I said.

"I might be in your lap all night."

I waggled my eyebrows at her. "You might want to change into a skirt, then."

She chuckled. "Don't tempt me, big man."

I kissed her again, then we donned our shoes and headed into the fray.

TWELVE

Harmony

I GRIPPED JAXON'S hand as we walked into the hotel restaurant, but he released me when we approached the group. I frowned up at him and linked my fingers with his again. He squeezed my hand and gave me a little smirk.

"Mine," I whispered, and he chuckled.

"Yeah, Rufus, yours."

"Then, we're gonna show it."

"Yeah?" I nodded and he cocked his head.

"This is all on your timeline, Harmony."

"I love you. I want to make that official."

"Okay, baby, we'll make it official." He kissed me gently, then we headed into the group.

I was suddenly surrounded by two incredibly gorgeous women and pulled away from Jaxon. "I'm Kim," the one said. "I belong to Knight. He's the giant one in between Jax and Ace. This is Cassidy. She belongs to Ace."

Kim was tall…model tall, and she was a stunning brunette. She wore a short skirted and slinky dress, complete with thigh-high boots, and all I could think was that I'd kill for her legs.

Cassidy was petite with curly blonde hair and she had a ready smile. She wore dark skinny jeans, a long-sleeved T-shirt, and a pair of black booties that gave her a little bit of height. Jaxon mentioned she was a ballerina and she was certainly as graceful as one.

"How did you and Jax meet?" Cassidy asked, guiding me to a chair toward the head of the table.

I took a seat and bit my lip. I wasn't sure how much I could tell them. "I'm—"

"You know I love you both dearly," Jaxon said, forcing his way between us. "But you're gonna have to leave the interrogation for another time."

"There was no interrogating," Cassidy countered.

"By you, I believe," Jaxon said, nodding toward Kim. "Kim, not so much."

"Hey. I resemble that remark."

Knight wrapped his arm around her waist and kissed the back of her neck. "The nineties called, they want their joke back." He reached in front of her and held his hand out. "I'm Knight."

I shook his hand. "It's nice to meet you."

Ace was next, and then he took Cassidy to sit across from me and Jaxon. My sister still hadn't arrived, but that didn't surprise me. I figured she'd make a grand entrance once everyone else arrived.

Mack and Darien walked in just before Brock and a blonde woman who could be the long lost Morgan sister. The couple was followed by Dallas and a stunning redhead who laughed at something he said, even though he appeared somewhat stone-faced.

I leaned closer to Jaxon. "Everything okay with Dallas?"

"Probably not."

"Really?"

"He can get a little wound up," Jaxon explained. "Especially, when it comes to Macey. He doesn't like not knowing every escape route available to him when he's with her."

"Uh oh."

"Put it out of your mind, Rufus. He'll get over it. Macey'll sort him out."

I squeezed his knee and smiled. "I appreciate how even keeled you are."

He chuckled. "We're still in the honeymoon stage, baby. You'll probably change your mind on that one."

He stood and took my hand, pulling me up and leading me to where Dallas and Brock were. I was introduced to Bailey and Macey, and then Jaxon wrapped an arm around my waist and pulled me against him.

"Everything good?" he asked Dallas.

"Dallas has his period," Macey said, and I bit back a laugh.

"Jesus Christ, Macey," he growled.

"*Or*…we can get a drink and enjoy a rare night together," she countered, sliding her hand into Dallas's back pocket. "Sound good?"

He studied her for a few seconds, then nodded.

She beamed up at him. "There's my man."

"Everyone's here!" Melody said in a sing-song voice, and any and all conversation was shut down while she played court. Butchy hovered, along with two of his team, and I smiled at him over the small crowd.

There was another man close to Lyric who I deduced was Matt, particularly when all the brothers hugged and ribbed each other for a good ten minutes or so. Once Jaxon introduced me to him, we took our seats again and everyone entered into a surprisingly relaxed evening.

* * *

Jaxon

"You got a minute?" Matt asked me.

"Yeah," I said, and squeezed the back of Harmony's neck. "Be right back."

She nodded and went back to her conversation with Lyric. I followed Matt away from the table and by the front door. "What's up?"

"Something's off," he said.

"With?"

"Julien."

"Butchy?" I clarified, and Matt nodded.

"He's wound up tighter than normal tonight. He's also been disappearing for long periods of time. Brock's thinking he's got a partner." Matt crossed his arms. "I don't like it. We need to keep an eye on him."

"Yeah, okay."

He smiled. "You and Harmony good?"

"Yeah, we're great."

"Good to see you happy, Jax."

I grinned. "Thanks, brother."

We headed back to the table and I noticed Harmony was gone and my heart raced. "Where's Harmony?" I asked no one in particular.

"She went somewhere with Butchy," Melody said, returning to her conversation with Billy.

"Where?" I snapped.

"Huh?"

"Where did they go?" I demanded, and I heard chairs scrape the ground, immediately knowing my team were already getting prepared.

"Probably upstairs. He had some video footage or something to show her."

"Fuck," I snapped, and headed for the lobby of the hotel.

* * *

Harmony

"Do you really think you got the guy on video?" I asked Butchy as we headed toward the elevators.

"I do," he said, settling his hand on my lower back.

"Did you show it to Matt?" I asked.

Butchy nodded. "Yeah. He wants you to see

172

if you recognize him."

"Okay." I smiled up at him as we stepped into a car. "I really want all of this to be over."

He smiled. "It will be."

As soon as the doors closed, I felt a pinch on my arm.

"Ouch!" I squeaked, then everything went black.

* * *

Jaxon

"You need to back down, Jax," Matt warned.

"She's been gone for twenty-two minutes," I hissed.

"And we're gonna find her," Brock said. "But you're way too close to this, brother. Let us do our job."

I dragged my hands through my hair and tried to figure out where she was. Her phone was off, or destroyed, so we couldn't trace her that way, which made things extremely difficult.

"I can't believe I didn't fuckin' see it," I snarled.

My brother settled his hand on my shoulder. "You weren't working this, Jax. If you'd been here, you probably would have figured it out before I did."

"You were the one who figured out it was her

being stalked, not Melody," Brock reminded me. "We worked this from that angle because of that. We'll find her."

"Sir?"

I raised my head to see a young man in a hotel uniform walk up to Matt and hand him a piece of paper. Matt shook his hand, then got on his phone, and I stood and made my way to him.

"Yeah?" he smiled. "You're amazing, Del. I owe you. I can do that. Okay, buddy. Bye." Matt slid his phone in his pocket and nodded. "Cameras caught Butchy's SUV heading to Gresham. Del got the license plate and is tracking him. He'll update us as we go."

I nodded. "Let's go."

* * *

Harmony

I came awake slowly, my arm on fire, but not just from the shot. I was currently lying on it, sideways in a moving vehicle. I stayed as still as possible, not wanting Butchy to know I was awake. I had no idea what the hell was going on or why I was here, but I realized in that second that Jaxon had been right, and I was the target all along.

I forced back tears and tried to look around. I couldn't get my bearings lying down in the back of the SUV, even if I was familiar with the vehicle. I felt the car slow down, so I closed my eyes again and tried to slow my breathing.

I heard a door open and close, registering behind my eyelids the inside light turn on. The door slammed and I waited a few seconds before peeking just a little. I was alone. This was my chance. I shifted slightly and realized my ankles were bound. I glanced down my body and groaned. My ankles were shackled and on top of that, they were handcuffed to the door. Even if I could get out, I wouldn't get anywhere unless I could take the panel off.

Shit.

I felt my pockets and confirmed my phone was gone. That would be the first thing Butchy would have gotten rid of and it was the only way Jaxon would be able to track me. A door popped open again, so I resumed my position, and tried my best to play possum.

"She's still out?"

Graham?

"Yeah," Butchy said.

"She should have woken up by now."

"I added a little to her dose."

"Why the fuck would you do that?" Graham snapped. "You coulda killed her."

My mind spun as I tried to figure out why Graham would be involved in any of this. I still couldn't figure out why Butchy was. We were friends. Close friends. God, I'd misjudged him.

"You don't think I know everything about her, including how much of anything she can tolerate?" Butchy seethed. "None of this would be happening if she hadn't forced those assholes on us. I'm her head of security. *Me.*"

"Okay, baby, calm down."

Baby? Oh, my god, they're in a relationship?

Now I was even more confused.

Butchy was sleeping with my sister, Graham was sleeping with Billy, and now it would seem Butchy and Graham were sleeping with each other as well.

Jesus, I'm stuck in my very own soap opera nightmare.

"Don't tell me to calm down. This is my plan and just because the timeline had been pushed up a little, it doesn't change a thing," Butchy shouted.

"Will you lower your voice?" Graham replied and their voices became too low for me to make out what they were saying. Whatever it was sounded heated and didn't last for long.

The driver's door slammed, the car started moving again and I tried to think of a way out. I could hear Butchy muttering to himself angrily but couldn't make out the words over the road noise as he drove. It was night and the windows of the SUV were tinted as dark as possible so there was no way I could signal any passing drivers without alerting Butchy.

My eyes burned as I desperately scanned the back of the SUV for something to aid in my escape, but the vehicle's all-black interior wasn't helping. It also didn't help that the Escalade was showroom fresh, therefore devoid of any loose items lying around that might be useful.

Butchy's muttering increased in volume and intensity and I flinched as he slammed his hand down on the steering wheel. Fortunately, Butchy didn't appear to notice my involuntary movement as he raged on in the darkness of the SUV's cab. Whatever he and Graham had been arguing about had clearly got him worked up, which meant he wasn't paying attention to me.

"This is my plan! I put all of this together!" Butchy shouted angrily.

A streetlight beamed through the window, catching the corner of a box hidden underneath the driver's seat. It could've easily been missed if I hadn't been laying at the exact angle I was, as it, like everything else in the Escalade, was black. I waited until Butchy's next outburst and reached underneath his seat as carefully as possible. My hand was barely able to reach it from where I was, but it felt like some sort of cardboard box. I pulled my hand back before Butchy could see me and waited for my next opportunity. I didn't have to wait long as Butchy's phone rang through the Escalade's hand's-free system.

"What is it now?" Butchy answered in a sharp tone.

"Don't be that way," Graham responded.

"Unless you've called to apologize, I'm not interested—"

"I'm sorry," Graham replied.

"I don't believe you," Butchy said, and I made my move. I stretched out my arm, extending my reach as far as possible without being detected. I was just barely able to grasp the end of the long, heavy box with my fingertips, and once I did, slowly pull it towards me.

"I'm not going to grovel, Butchy. I've said I'm sorry and you can choose to believe that I'm sincere or not."

Peeking down at the floor, I could now see it

was a decorative wine box, adorned with the Cadillac logo. No doubt a gift from the dealership, that was shoved under the seat, not to be seen again. Until now. Not that it would do me much good now. What was I going to do with it? Get Butchy drunk and make a break for it? Maybe I could hit him on the head with it. Knocking people out in the movies always looked so easy, but the lack of swinging room and by feet being bound made it feel like a risky move to try. However, right now it was the only plan I had.

"I'm doing all of this for you," Butchy said. "Months of planning, and you're being ungrateful."

"Don't act like this isn't everything you've ever wanted."

What in the hell were these two talking about?

As my head was clearing, my panic was increasing. As a certified control freak, this was my worst possible nightmare. I was at the mercy of two insane men. Men with a plan. A plan that involved me, yet I knew nothing about.

"But I'm doing it now and in this way for you."

"All I'm saying is this isn't all about me," Graham said. "You're getting what you want out of this as well. That's the point of this whole thing."

"Fine. Apology accepted," Butchy said.

"I'll meet you at our spot as soon as I'm done here. *Don't start without me*."

"I know."

"I mean it, Butchy. Don't lay a hand on her until I get there."

A chill ran up my spine and I fought back the urge to cry.

"The drugs should wear off right around the time we reach the cabin. If she wakes up any sooner, I'll hit her with another shot. So far, there hasn't been a peep from Sleeping Beauty," Butchy said, casually glancing back at me.

"She'll be peeping soon enough…is your car clean?" Graham asked abruptly.

"You see. It's those kinds of questions that make my blood boil. I'm the head of a private security company. Do you honestly think I wouldn't have already disabled my own car's GPS and emergency services?"

"I know you're the best at what you do. I just get worried sometimes because this one is more than just a job to you. This one is personal, and when things get personal…mistakes can happen."

I laid perfectly still, my eyes shut, my heart pounding so loud I could barely hear what

Butchy said next.

"I've waited for this for a long time and I want this to last as long as possible. I'm going to make sure Harmony Morgan experiences every possible emotion and sensation a human being can feel, all by my hand."

"And once you're done with her?" Graham asked.

"Why do you have to make this all about you?"

"She's been your obsession for too long and you'll never fully be mine as long as your fantasies about her continue. So, for the next forty-eight hours you can rape and torture her all you want, but once you're done…"

"She's yours," Butchy answered.

"Mine to *what*? I need to hear you say it."

"To kill."

THIRTEEN

Jaxon

"**D**AMMIT! HE DEFINITELY disabled her phone," I growled as I scanned for Harmony's current location. I wasn't really surprised, given that Butchy is a security expert and he'd likely disabled his own car's GPS as well. "How the hell are we going to find her?" I asked as Matt and I hurried to the car.

"Hold on one second," Matt said, before

turning and running back to Brock, who he'd ordered to stay behind with Melody and Lyric. After only a few seconds, Matt returned carrying Brock's laptop. "Let's go," he said.

"Where?" I asked. "They could be headed anywhere."

"This will help, get in the car," Matt replied, holding up the laptop as we moved.

"I'm driving," I said, and Matt knew better than to argue with me.

We got in the car and I peeled out into the street, toward the direction of the nearest freeway exchange. "Which way?" I asked Matt, who was looking intently at the laptop's screen. "Matt! Where am I going?" I shouted in frustration.

"It looks like they're on I-5, headed for Vancouver," Matt shouted.

"How do you know that. What the hell are you looking at?"

"Brock is not only a Boy Scout, but he runs up my annual budget every year with the latest in surveillance gear. After being assigned to this case, the first thing he did was outfit every vehicle Melody Morgan rode in on a regular basis. Per our SOPs, the existence and placements of these trackers was on a need-to-know basis, and Brock never felt like Butchy needed to know."

"And now we know exactly where they are," I said, increasing my already dangerous speed.

"You can buy Brock a beer later, if you don't get us both killed with your driving."

I appreciated Matt's attempt at keeping me cool, but my skin felt like it was on fire. If I didn't find Harmony before Butchy... I couldn't even allow myself to think of what that creep was capable of. I also didn't have the time to hate myself for not seeing the signs. I'd be sure to tear into myself once I had Harmony back in the one place I knew she was safe.

My arms.

* * *

Harmony

And so finally, I knew everything. The identity of the stalker, who he was after, and what his ultimate plan was. I also knew I was soon to face unimaginable horrors at the hands of a pure psychopath only to be killed by another psychopath. The only thing greater than my fear at that moment, was the desire to escape this car. To somehow fight my way to freedom and back to Jaxon. As afraid as I was for my own life, I was also afraid for his, because I knew if Butchy succeeded with his plans, Jaxon would be broken. I also knew he'd leave a trail of dead bodies in his wake in a thirst for vengeance.

"I'll see you at the cabin and make sure no one is following you," Butchy said before hanging up.

"You still asleep, my pet?" Butchy asked and I felt the cold steel of what felt like a gun barrel poke into my sternum. This was one of the most sensitive areas in the human body as the skin is very thin, directly over bone. It's why doctors tap this area when trying to revive unconscious patients. It's very difficult not to react when this area is poked. Difficult but not impossible and when you have sisters, it's a skill that becomes required very early on. My sisters and I would viciously poke, pull, and pinch every sensitive area on each other, and reacting to such assaults was the ultimate sign of weakness.

Butchy, satisfied I was still out cold, returned to the road. "Good. It's best you get your rest. You're certainly going to need it."

His tone made my flesh crawl. It took everything I had not to react, but I knew I had to be stronger than my fear if I had even a sliver of chance at making it out of this situation alive.

"You know…" Butchy continued. "Maybe I will give you just a little more ketamine when I stop at the service road gate. I'd hate for you to wake up too early and give me any trouble getting you out of the car. More importantly, we don't want you to prove Mr. Know-it-all right."

The wine bottle to the head plan was my only option. I'd wait for him to stop at a traffic light and I'd hit him as hard as I could. Maybe then I could flag a passing motorist or find an open business. I had no idea what our current location was, but civilization couldn't be too far away.

"I may as well put on some music since we'll be on the highway for a while," Butchy said out loud before turning on some kind of operatic music.

So much for stoplights.

I was going to have to make my move as soon as possible, even if that meant while we were still moving. I made another reach for the box and was able to pull it all the way to me and flip it open. As I suspected, the box contained a bottle of wine, a small 'thank you' card, and something else that caught my eye. A stainless-steel folding corkscrew.

I slowly and carefully reached down and picked up the corkscrew and laid back down, praying the whole time that Butchy wouldn't see me. Fortunately, he was busy singing along, giving me the opportunity to unfold the corkscrew and secure a firm grip around it in my right hand. The song, approaching its climax, swelled as the volume of Butchy's caterwauling also increased. Butchy steered with his left hand as he fully extended his right, holding out the final note of the song's melody. As soon as the song ended, Butchy's arm dropped, fully exposing the right side of his neck. I pulled myself up with all my upper body strength and jabbed the corkscrew into his neck as hard as I could.

I'm not sure if the task was easier than I'd intended, or if the quality and sharpness of the thank you gift were simply top notch, but the corkscrew plunged into his neck with ease. At his attempt to move away from the pain, the weapon was ripped out, causing blood to spray all over the interior. Butchy screamed and his hand went to his neck as he jerked at the wheel, causing us to swerve violently all over the road.

"You bitch!" Butchy yelled as blood pumped through the open gash in his neck.

The traffic was light but we were by no means alone, and I was terrified that the SUV would swerve into another car, injuring someone. Before I could think about that much further, I came down on Butchy once more with the corkscrew, this time hitting his ear as I did, tearing off a huge chunk of it before plunging once again into his neck. This time Butchy lost consciousness and the SUV immediately pulled to the left, causing us to crash into the center median and spin out of control before coming to a stop in the middle of the highway. The vehicle's front and side airbags deployed, one of which hit me, knocking me unconscious.

* * *

Jaxon

I could barely see the tail lights of Butchy's Escalade as I hung back as far as possible. There weren't many people traveling I-5 toward Woodland this time of night, and I didn't want to give Butchy any reasons for suspicion. I had to keep my cool and make sure I gave him no cause for alarm. No sudden moves whatsoever.

Just then, the SUV took a sharp left into the concrete divider, crashing violently into it before spinning like a top in the center of the highway. I put the gas pedal to the floor and raced to the scene to find broken glass, steam and blood everywhere.

"Fuck!" I bellowed, and shot out of the car, running as fast as I could for Harmony.

* * *

Harmony

"Harmony! Baby, can you hear me?"

I heard Jaxon's voice as though he were calling to me through a long, empty tunnel. The only light I could see was a single pinhole directly in the center of my field of vision, and it burned with such white-hot intensity that I thought for a moment that I might be dead. Is that why I could hear Jaxon's voice in the distance? Was I dying and leaving him behind? Or had Butchy succeeded and killed Jaxon too? Were we both dead and in heaven together?

The sharp pain in my ankle let me know that I was certainly not in heaven, and very much alive. As my eyes continued to open, the tell-tale nausea and agonizing headache associated with a hard hit to the head swamped me.

"Harmony!" Jax's voice caused me to focus on him and it really was him. He was leaning over me and examining me for injuries. "Are you shot? Did he stab you?" Jaxon cried out.

"No, this is...his blood." I pointed to the driver's seat, where Butchy laid slumped over the steering wheel.

"You don't have to worry about him anymore," Jaxon said.

"Did I...? Is he dead?"

"Not yet. But he's bleeding out and it might take a while for the paramedics to arrive way out here. I've handcuffed him to the steering wheel so he's not going anywhere. Don't worry about him. All I care about is you and that you're okay. Let's get you out of here." Jaxon began to lift me out of the SUV, but I cried out in pain.

"My ankle. I think it might be broken. He tied me to the inside door handle."

"That sonofabitch," Jaxon seethed, and my thoughts once again went to visions of scorched earth had Butchy and Graham's plans been carried out. "Hold on, I'll come around to the other side and free you," Jaxon said.

"Graham," I said.

"What about him?" Jaxon asked, puzzled.

"He's been working with Butchy this whole time."

"Yeah, baby, we know."

"You do?"

"Yeah. Intel came down while we were at dinner. How did you find out?" he asked.

"I heard them talking and fighting about what they were going to do with me. It was all some sort of twisted lover's quarrel between them," I explained.

"Lover's quarrel?"

"Apparently, Butchy's been obsessed with me for years, but Graham agreed to let Butchy rape and torture me if he got to kill me in return. They were going to use me as some sort of sick way of proving their love for each other."

"Jesus, the intel didn't go *that* deep."

I bit back tears. "I was so scared, Jaxon."

"We'll find Graham. I promise. You don't have anything to worry about any more," he said, freeing me from my restraints before lifting me out of the car and kissing my temple. "I'm gonna get you to the hospital so they can check you out."

"I'm okay, Jax. I just want to sleep."

"I need you not to do that, Rufus."

"I don't have a concussion, honey."

"Did you pass out?"

"Um…"

"Exactly. Humor me," he growled.

"Okay," I whispered.

I heard sirens as Jaxon settled me gently into his SUV, reaching over and buckling me in. "Do not fall asleep. I'm gonna talk to the cops real quick then take you to the hospital."

"I'll try," I promised, just as Jaxon put his

phone to his ear.

"Yeah, he's handcuffed to his steering wheel. Ambulance is pulling up now." He turned and raised his chin. "Yeah, brother, I see you. Okay. Thanks."

Jaxon jogged around the hood of his car and climbed in. "Matt's handling everything from here. Let's get you fixed up."

"Isn't it illegal to leave the scene of an accident?"

"I'll take the hit, baby."

He pulled onto the freeway and drove me to Legacy emergency, carrying me inside as I tried to keep from screaming out. Now that the adrenaline had worn off, I was in more pain than I'd ever experienced in my life, and with every step he made, it felt like spikes were being dug into my ankle.

A nurse brought a wheelchair and Jaxon set me as gently as he could into it. I couldn't stop myself from whimpering as he lifted my foot into the footrest, jarring my ankle. "I'm going to be sick."

The nurse was quick on the draw and handed me a plastic bag attached to a round carboard thingy. I aimed the best I could, puking into the small opening.

As I answered the questions Jaxon asked

while filling out admittance paperwork, we waited in the emergency area until I was called down to radiology.

"Baby, don't fall asleep."

"I'm so tired."

"I know. We need to get you checked out first."

"Harmony?" a nurse called from the doorway behind me.

Jaxon stood and wheeled me toward her, following her down the hallway and into another waiting area.

"A tech will be in shortly," she said, and left us alone.

I reached for Jaxon and squeezed his hand as a sharp pain shot through my ankle. "I need morphine."

"We'll get you—"

A man in blue scrubs walked in and stalled. "I'm Kevin and I'll be taking your images today. You're in a lot of pain, huh?" he asked.

"She needs something," Jaxon demanded.

"Let's get your scans done and we'll get you a room so the doc can get you sorted." He gave me a gentle smile. "I'm fast, Miss Morgan. I promise this won't take long."

"Come with me," I begged Jaxon.

"Yeah, baby, I'm right behind you."

True to his word, Kevin was quick. My ankle was x-rayed, then my head was CAT scanned, and I was in a room with in fifteen minutes. A doctor came in five minutes later and I was dosed with morphine and all was better with the world.

I couldn't have too much in the way of pain meds because of the concussion, but it was certainly enough to take the edge off the pain in my ankle...and make me very emotional.

"I can't believe you found me," I sobbed as Jaxon pushed out of the chair he was in and slid onto the bed next to me, pulling me gently against his chest.

"I can't believe you doubted me."

"I didn't doubt that you'd try, but Butchy disabled all the GPS and tracker stuff on the SUV, so I didn't know if you'd be able to do it."

He stroked my cheek. "I will always find you, Rufus. Never ever forget that."

"I won't." I burrowed into his chest. "I love you so much, Jaxon, I thought I'd never see you again."

"You can't get rid of me that easily."

I met his eyes and smiled through my tears. "You realize you're stuck with me now. I'll never let you go."

He chuckled. "I'm countin' on that, baby."

"Like, no break up, no divorce. Just death. If

you try to leave me… not a hair, not a fiber."

"Oh, yeah?"

"Yeah, my man's a badass FBI man, I'm gonna learn all I need to know about how to bury a body if I need to."

He laughed. "Jesus, Rufus, you're diabolical on morphine."

I snuggled back against him. "And don't you forget it."

He lifted my chin and kissed me gently. "Really glad you're feeling better, baby."

"Are you in more pain?" the doctor asked as he walked back in.

"No, I'm fine," I said.

"If that changes, you let me know. We got your scans back. Your concussion's not too bad, so you're good there. Your ankle on the other hand…" He logged into the computer and turned the screen toward me. "You've got a nasty break," he said, showing me the x-ray. "When did you last eat?"

"Six hours ago?" I asked, glancing at Jaxon.

"Closer to seven," he corrected.

"Okay," the doctor said. "We will plan on surgery first thing in the morning. You can't eat or drink anything until after, which won't be fun, sorry. But it should be a pretty straight-forward fix, so you'll be out of here in a couple of days."

"I'm so thirsty," I said.

The doctor checked his watch and nodded. "You can have some water now, but only ice chips after one a.m."

This meant I had about an hour to drink as much water as I could. "Okay, thank you."

"Do you have any questions for me?"

I shook my head.

"Okay, we'll get you settled in a room upstairs and keep you comfortable for the night, then tomorrow, we'll get your ankle fixed."

"Thanks, doctor," I said, and he left us again.

Jaxon filled a pitcher with ice and water and I swear nothing had ever tasted better. Once I was moved into a private room, I was left to rest, although Jaxon was at my beck and call all night, making sure I had ice chips and pain killers.

By the time I was wheeled away for surgery, I was pretty sure he was dead on his feet, while I'd slept like a baby.

"Go home, honey," I said. "Get some rest."

"Not gonna happen." He kissed me gently and watched me roll away.

Harmony

Two weeks later…

I HOPPED IN place as I zipped up the last of my bags, then sat on the edge of the bed and stared at the spare bedroom I'd called home for the last eight years. I'd been here one week every summer, then Thanksgiving and Christmas, but otherwise, I was on the road with Melody. I didn't even feel sad that I was leaving and that made me melancholic. At this stage in my life, I should have more roots.

At least I got some home time now. Graham was still out there somewhere, and since his home was in Salem and his life was there as well, Jaxon wanted me as far away as possible to let his team do a deep dive with me out of the way. I had a feeling when we got home, I'd be back to being watched twenty-four-seven.

Home.

Wow, when did that happen?

Oh, I know. The second Jaxon told me he loved me, I knew I'd found home.

I smiled. He'd made everything right.

After a conversation with Melody, she'd informed me that she had plans to talk to me about firing Butchy…until he seduced her into keeping him. She'd admitted she didn't like the attention he was paying me and had said as much to him. Once again, I was clueless to his obsession. But this fact brought a lot of things into focus and also made me sad for my sister. She was always being seduced into doing something for someone. And when I say that, I don't just mean a sexual seduction. Despite her status as one of the most beautiful women in the world, she was also one of the most insecure and bad people preyed on that.

I hoped one day she'd find herself so that she could find her 'happy.'

"Last one?" Jaxon asked from the doorway. I nodded, and he stepped into the room. "Hey, you okay?"

"Yes. I just feel a little…I don't know, disconnected." I slid my arms around his waist as he lifted me further onto the bed. I was supposed to keep my leg elevated, but I was never good at doing nothing. "I have never had anything of my own, if that makes sense. I lived with my parents, then my sister, and now…I don't know."

"With me."

I shook my head and met his eyes. "I don't want to do that."

He frowned. "Okay."

"It's too soon," I explained. "I need to have some of my own space for a while. I need to know you longer before we move in together."

"Okay, baby, I can get behind that."

"But I'd love to stay with you while I look for a place."

He grinned. "You trust me not to sabotage your attempts?"

I patted his chest. "I'll have to, I guess."

He leaned down and kissed me gently. "You promised me a tour of Savannah."

"I did." I reached up and stroked his cheek.

"I wish we could walk."

"There is a wheelchair downstairs," he reminded me.

"No way in hell."

I just couldn't fathom him wheeling me around like an invalid. I suppose, technically, I was, but I wasn't ready to admit defeat yet.

Jaxon cupped my face. "In that case, Rufus, you promised me a fountain."

I rolled my eyes. "Okay, big man, let's go see the fountain."

Lyric's home was less than a block from Forsyth Park, in the historic district, and I was honestly a little jealous I didn't own it myself. It had been built in 1860 and had been a wreck, but Lyric spent two years restoring it to its current beauty and it was now worth more than three times what she paid for it eight years ago.

After parking close by, Jaxon grabbed my crutches, and we hobbled around the fountain for a few minutes, and then Jaxon saw a horse and buggy go by and he decided we were going to have an adventure.

"You want to do a tour?" I asked.

"Yeah."

I grinned wide. Living here meant I never took advantage of anything touristy. I was too busy reconnecting with my sisters when I was home, rather than exploring, so the opportunity to see my city with the sexiest man alive made me positively giddy. It also meant we didn't have to see Savannah from the cage of a car.

"I take it you've never done it?" Jaxon asked, and I shook my head.

"Never."

He wrapped his arms around me and hugged me tight. "I'm glad I can pop your cherry, then."

I chuckled. "Oh my god, Jax, stop, or I'm gonna suck you off in front of this fountain."

"Jesus," he hissed, kissing me gently. "You're going to kill me."

"You'll die happy, though."

He laughed. "Hell, yeah, I will."

I settled on a bench and pulled my phone out of my pocket. "I'm going to see if I can make a reservation."

"Always prepared," he mused.

"Damn straight."

I booked a reservation for later in the afternoon, then took Jaxon to my favorite bistro before he insisted we go for ice cream.

"We've only got ten minutes before our tour," I pointed out.

"After, then."

"I can't keep eating like this, honey. I'll gain a thousand pounds."

He smiled gently, leaning down to kiss me. "More of you to love, then."

"We better go, Jax. I'm losing my resolve."

He chuckled, taking my hand and kissing me one more time, then he carried me to our buggy ride.

* * *

"Did you do the ghost tour?" Lyric asked as we carried food to the table. Lyric had cooked an old-fashioned southern meal tonight, complete with grits, and my stomach grumbled with anticipation.

"There's a ghost tour?" Jaxon asked, pouring wine.

"Yes, there is and no we did not," I said. "But we can before we leave on Sunday if you want to."

"I don't know how it could top today's, so maybe we save it for next time."

"Are you telling me you're not going to take my sister away forever?" Lyric asked hopefully.

He smiled gently. "I would never take your sister away from you, Lyric."

"Will you come for Christmas?"

"I can't promise Christmas," he said. "My brothers' club does a shit ton over the holidays, and I'm kind of committed to that every year, but how about you come over the holidays and we'll come any other time of the year."

I kind of melted and couldn't stop a smile. "Aw, look at my two favorite people making plans for the future."

Jaxon slid his arm around my waist and kissed my temple. "You *can* weigh in here, Rufus, if you disagree."

"I know. But so far you haven't said anything I need to verbally spank you for."

He chuckled and we sat down to eat after he propped my foot up on the chair next to me... just as Melody breezed in.

"Hello, bitches!" she cooed as she waltzed into the dining room and flopped into a chair.

"Um, hi," Lyric said. "Welcome home."

"Thanks." Melody headed into the kitchen to grab a place setting and wine glass before returning and piling food onto her plate.

I glanced at Lyric, who shrugged.

"Um, DiDi?" I leaned toward her. "What are you doing here?"

"The movie's over."

I squeezed my eyes shut briefly. "I know, honey, but you start a tour next week. Aren't you supposed to be in Atlanta for rehearsals?"

"I didn't want to go. I wanted to come home for a little while." She took a bite of grits and let out a moan of pleasure. "You always make the best grits, LiLi."

"Thank you," she said, and sighed. "Eat your dinner and then you and I are going to sit down and figure out what the hell is really going on, okay?"

"No, we really don't need to," Melody countered.

"What did you do?" I asked, then added, "Nope, never mind. I don't need to know."

Lyric gasped and I turned to see her scrolling through her phone. "Oh my god, woman, you *didn't*."

Melody took a big bite of grits and studied her plate.

"What?" I asked.

"Shall I share, baby sister?" Lyric threatened. "Or would you rather talk privately?"

Melody used her fork to indicate she was busy eating.

"Fine," Lyric said. "Melody has managed to get caught in another sex tape scandal. This time with Jason Maxx."

I groaned. "Did Jason know you were filming him?"

"Um, he was filming me," Melody countered.

"Oh, so a little different than with Bam," I said with a sneer.

Bam Nelson was the drummer for Roses for Anna, currently one of the biggest bands in the world. He and Melody had dated for a few months before she had fucked it up and released a sex tape, furthering her career, but ruining any chance for a meaningful relationship.

Melody wrinkled her nose. "A *lot* different."

"Did you and Jason decide to release this together?" Lyric asked.

"If we did?"

Lyric threw her hands in the air. "Well, then you're on your own. I'm not cleaning this up."

"Did I ask you to?"

Lyric closed her eyes and took two deep breaths. "Okay, sissy, I'm taking my manager hat off and putting my sister hat on, because I'd like to spend the next few days with Melody the normal human, not Melody the psycho porn star."

I bit back a snort as Melody grinned wide. "Movies and ice cream?"

"Yes, dearheart, movies and ice cream," Lyric confirmed.

Jaxon leaned over and whispered, "I can make myself scarce if you need some sister time."

I smiled. "This is why I love you best."

He chuckled and kissed my cheek before focusing back on his food.

With a girls' night in planned, we finished dinner, and Jaxon headed upstairs to work while I changed into PJs to hang with my sisters. Of course, Jaxon pretty much had to carry me downstairs and settle me on the sofa, but then he made himself scarce.

* * *

Jaxon

I had just hung up with Brock when a knock came at the bedroom door. I pulled it open to find Lyric and I frowned. "Everything okay."

"Oh, yes. But NiNi's sacked out on the sofa. She had pretty much an entire bottle of wine. Figured you'd want to know, so you didn't worry."

"She shouldn't be drinking…"

"She said she hasn't had anything harder than ibuprofen, so I didn't stop her."

"Yeah, I guess that's true." I smiled. "So she had fun."

"We all did. It was much needed, so thank you for helping to facilitate that."

"Don't know that I can take any credit."

"You could have whisked her away and showed her a good time, but you didn't, so…"

I chuckled. "Maybe so."

"Anyway, I'm going to fall into bed now. I'm too old for junk food and copious amounts of

206

booze."

"I'll go check on Harmony. Sleep well."

"Thanks. You too."

Lyric headed off to her room and I made my way downstairs to see if I could rouse my woman. She was curled up on the huge sofa, a blanket wrapped around her and her hair covering her face. I reached down and slid her golden locks gently away and stroked her cheek. Jesus, she was beautiful.

I gathered her into my arms and lifted her, and she sighed as she looped her arms around my neck and burrowed against me. "Hi."

"Hey, baby. I heard you had fun."

"*So* much fun," she breathed out. "I'm a little drunk."

I smiled. "I heard that, too."

"I had wine," she whispered as I carried her upstairs.

"I know."

She slid her face into my neck and pressed her lips to my pulse. "Wine makes me horny."

I walked into her room and set her feet on the floor. "You've mentioned that before."

She bit her lip and smiled up at me. She wore pink fluffy pajamas with horses all over them, and I noticed that Lyric had been wearing the same. So fuckin' cute how they wore matching

PJs and had a girls' night, and now she knelt in front of me and fumbled with the zipper on my jeans.

"Baby—"

"I swear to god, if you try to tell me I'm too drunk to suck you off, I'll be really pissed."

"You can't even get my zipper down," I pointed out. "And I don't want you hurting your ankle."

"Then help me, big man, because I want your dick in my mouth, pronto."

"I'm not doing this if you're not going to remember," I argued.

"Oh, I'm gonna remember," she rasped, managing to free me from my jeans and dragging them down my legs. I lifted her onto the edge of the mattress so she could take the weight off her leg, then her mouth was wrapped around my dick and I was weaving my fingers into her hair. Fuck, it was perfect.

* * *

Harmony

I took Jaxon deeper, stroking his shaft with one hand while cupping his balls with the other. God, he tasted incredible and I couldn't get enough.

"Now, baby," he grunted and I gripped his thighs, as he stiffened and came in my mouth.

I took every ounce, swallowing as he hooked his hands under my arms and pulled me up, kissing me gently. "Your turn."

I grinned. "I love it when it's my turn."

After helping me out of my PJs, he removed the rest of his clothing and pulled the comforter down, guiding me under the covers. Kissing his way down my body, he covered my core with his mouth and I lifted my knees and arched to get closer. I wove my fingers into his hair as he licked and sucked his way around my pussy, grabbing a pillow to scream into as an orgasm washed over me.

He moved back up my body, linking his fingers with mine and sliding slowly into me. I whimpered with need as he buried himself deeper and deeper, then slammed into me over and over again, careful not to jar my leg.

"Jax," I rasped, biting his shoulder to keep from crying out. "Oh, god, get there, baby."

I hooked my good leg around his waist in an effort to get closer and he thrust twice, then let out a quiet grunt and I felt his dick pulse inside of me as I came, and came hard.

Keeping our connection, he rolled us onto our sides and I sighed in pleasure. "That was perfection."

"It always is with you," he said, stroking my

cheek.

I noticed his shoulder and gasped. The bite wound was angry and red and I felt horrible. "Oh, honey, I'm sorry. I think I might have broken your skin."

He smiled. "Kinda dig it, Rufus."

"You dig it when your girlfriend wounds you during sex?"

He ran a finger over my collarbone. "It's sexy how you get all primal."

I rolled my eyes. "Well, I suppose that's an accurate description. You kind of drive me wild."

He kissed me again. "I found you a place to rent if you want it."

"You did?"

"Yep. Kim's got a place in the Pearl. She just had a renter vacate and will rent month-to-month."

"Seriously?"

"Yeah, baby. Seriously."

I smiled. "Is it nice?"

"Considering the fact she's loaded and has impeccable taste, yeah, Rufus, it's nice. It has some pretty kick-ass water views."

"And I can afford it?"

He chuckled. "You absolutely can afford it."

I sighed. "That makes things so much easier."

"Of course, you can still always move in with me."

"I know." I ran my thumb across his bottom lip, then kissed it. "I promise it'll happen eventually."

"No pressure, Rufus, just want you to know it's still an option."

I smiled. "I know. And just because I'm not ready to move in with you right now, doesn't mean I love you any less."

"Noted."

"Plus, you have a piano."

"Yes, I do. You are correct."

"If I don't play on a regular basis, I'll get rusty."

"No one wants that."

"No, we really don't," I agreed.

"I could always give you one of my keyboards," he said.

I smiled. "Explain to me why you have a piano and two keyboards when you don't play."

"I told you, instruments just seem to show up. I have the space, and I use all of them when I'm recording."

"This is true."

"I still expect a Morgan sisters serenade to-morrow."

"Okay, baby, I'll make it happen."

He kissed me again and then he went to clean up before climbing back into bed with me and holding me until I fell asleep.

Harmony

I STOOD IN the middle of Kim's giant condo overlooking the Willamette River and directed my moving muscle which consisted of Jaxon, his brothers Aidan and Carter, and Brock and Dallas. I, of course, was not allowed to lift anything, but I refused to sit on the chair Jaxon had brought over, so I was directing using my crutches to point.

I didn't have much in the way of large items,

but I did find a bed on Craigslist, along with a dresser and sofa, so they were getting moved and set up for me while I took time to stare out at the water whenever I could.

"Are you helping or gawking?" Jaxon accused.

"Both?" I grinned. "Sorry. It's just so pretty."

He nodded. "Yeah, it really is. I'm gonna order pizza, any requests?"

"Combination, please."

"Kim and Cassidy are bringing drinks, and they'll be here in twenty minutes according to Carter."

"That's so nice," I said. "I'll pay them back."

"No you won't," Carter said, walking into the room. "If you try, Cass'll freak."

"*I* should be covering all the costs. Y'all are helping *me* move."

"And my woman looks for an excuse to get us together every second she's breathing, and since you've just facilitated a way for that to happen, you won't get anywhere trying to pay her back." He headed to the kitchen and grabbed a couple of bottled waters from the fridge, before heading back into the bedroom.

Jaxon grinned. "The Quinns' have spoken."

I rolled my eyes. "I *will* find a way to pay them back, mark my words."

Jaxon chuckled, pulling out his phone. "Good luck with that."

"Are you going to give me an issue paying for the pizza as well?"

He grinned, waving his phone at me. "It's already done."

"We'll see," I retorted, and Jaxon let out a quiet grunt before kissing me quickly.

I had a feeling he'd make sure money never left my wallet, but I was still going to try.

Unsurprisingly, I failed.

"You want me to stay or go?" Jaxon asked, sitting next to me on the sofa.

"Stay, if that's okay."

He frowned. "You in pain?"

"Don't talk to me like you know me."

He sighed. "Where's the stuff?"

"The ibuprofen's in the cabinet above the microwave."

"I think you need something stronger, Rufus," he countered, standing and heading into the kitchen.

"Fine," I breathed out. "The vicodin's next to it."

He brought me back a pill and some water. "Why are you torturing yourself?"

"I'm not. I promise. I just don't like to take the hard stuff when the other works fine."

He raised an eyebrow, but didn't argue. "You want to take a bath?"

"Oh my god, yes. Do I have plastic bags?"

Kim had the coolest clawfoot tub that begged to be bathed in, and I'd mentioned that when she'd walked me through it a few days ago.

Jaxon smiled. "Yeah, baby, you do. I'll go get it started and then help you."

He kissed me quickly, then headed into the master bedroom. I followed him, hobbling with my crutches, and sitting on the edge of the bed. After helping me get naked, he wrapped my boot in a large trash bag, tying it closed, then taping it for extra protection.

"Ready?" he asked.

I nodded and he lifted me, setting me gently in the tub and I settled my leg over the side. Jaxon had folded a towel over the rim for comfort and I sighed as the warm water covered me. "This is heaven."

Jaxon grinned and set my body wash and shampoo on the ledge. "You're cute as hell with your plastic leg."

"You think so, huh?" I raised my leg slightly. "It's lavender scented which is the newest fashion accessory choice. Practical and pleasant smelling."

He laughed, leaning down to kiss me. "You

soak, I'm gonna do a little work. Call me when you're ready to get out."

"It will be never," I warned.

"Okay, Rufus, I'll drag you out when you start to prune."

"Wait until I'm fully shriveled, please."

"We'll see."

I flicked water at him and he laughed as he left the room.

* * *

Jaxon

I studied the information Brock had emailed me and sighed. This wasn't good. I pulled out my phone and called him and he answered on the first ring. "Matt thinks he might have a lead," Brock said.

"'Might' isn't making me feel better," I said. "I don't like that Graham's gone to ground. Where's Billy?"

"Still in Savannah."

"You're sure he's clean?"

"Squeaky," Brock said. "I think he was just as sideswiped by all of this as the Morgan sisters."

"Yeah, that's the impression I got as well."

"Did you see him in Savannah?"

"Hell, no. That man knew he needed to keep

a wide berth with me," I ground out. "I don't care that he's one of their best friends. He put that asshole directly in the path of Harmony and I'll never forgive him for that."

"Yeah," Brock said. "But love does weird things to people."

"Love should never blind you so much you forget who your friends are."

Brock chuckled. "This is true. You know, there is a possibility Graham's gone for good."

"Do you believe that?" I challenged.

"Not in the least."

I sighed. "Me neither."

"Kim's place is wired, and her doormen are vigilant, Jax. We've got guys on her when you're not with her. Harmony's covered."

"I wish that made me feel better."

"I get it, brother."

"Yeah, I know you do."

Brock had met his wife Bailey when she was in our protection. He'd fallen for her the second he'd met her, but because she was a 'job,' had tried to force down his feelings.

He'd failed.

"I just wish she'd stay with me," I admitted.

"I hear ya."

"Jax?" Harmony called.

"I need to go, brother," I said.

"Okay," Brock said. "If I hear anything, I'll let you know, but just try to relax for the moment."

"Easier said than done."

"No doubt," Brock agreed. "I'll talk to you later."

I hung up and headed back to the bathroom to help Harmony get out of the tub.

* * *

Harmony

Four weeks later…

"Your ankle looks great," Doctor Stone said, pulling up the new set of X-rays. "As long as you go slow and don't run any marathons for a few weeks, you can just wear the brace for another week, then you're good to go."

Doctor Stone was the older brother of Dallas Stone, one of Jaxon's partners in the FBI, and he was gorgeous. I mean, it made sense…Dallas was gorgeous, so of course, Alec would be, plus the doctor factor ratcheted it up a notch.

"So, no more crutches?"

He smiled. "No more crutches."

I beamed at Jaxon. "We can go shopping now."

"Yippee," he deadpanned, and Alec laughed.

I clapped my hands. "Let's go. Mama needs new plates."

"Jesus," Jaxon hissed, and I grinned taking his hand.

"Stop playing coy. I know you're just as excited as me."

"Oh, yeah. Hold me back."

"Well, you two have fun. Call me if you have any questions."

"Thanks Doc," Jaxon said.

I shook Alec's hand. "Yes, thank you."

Alec left us and Jaxon loaded me in the car and took me to the mall. We shopped for about an hour before Jaxon declared he'd had enough and it was time to eat.

"We could just eat here," I suggested.

"We're not eatin' at Derby's, Rufus. I'm gonna take you to a real restaurant."

"Wait, what's Derby's? You know, I want to experience *all* of the famous Portland eateries."

"Derby's food isn't so much famous, as it is infamous."

"What do you mean by that?"

"Well, let me ask you this… have you recently smoked a copious amount of marijuana?"

I laughed. "The devil's lettuce, why, no, I have not."

Jaxon smirked. "Then, if you are not friends

with either Cheech or Chong, Derby's would likely not be your first dining choice. We're not even sure they sell meat from a cow."

I grimaced. "Oh, well, what kind of meat is it?"

"I had a friend in high school who worked at a Derby's that swears they once received a shipment of boxes labeled, 'Beef.'"

"Why is that weird?"

"Because it wasn't spelled B-E-E-F."

"Oh, God, how was it spelled?"

He sighed. "I fear that by saying it out loud, it somehow loses its impact. B-E-E-P-H," he explained.

I dropped my head back and groaned. "Okay, the Pink Priest it is."

"I think we've had just about enough excitement for one day, don't you?"

"Maybe so."

"Rock Bottom, then."

"Perfect," I said.

He lifted my bags. "Did you leave anything in the stores?"

"Probably not."

He grinned. "How about I go get the car and pick you up? You need to get off your ankle."

"Thanks, honey."

I would have been surprised that he was leaving me alone, if even for a few minutes, but I knew there were a couple of Dogs of Fire recruits who were assigned to me twenty-four-seven. Even when Jaxon was with me, if we weren't at my place or his, we had a shadow.

We walked outside and Jaxon located our guard dog, Cheese, who was standing by his bike on his cell phone, gave him a chin lift, then headed for his SUV. I sat on the bench outside the mall entrance and scrolled through my phone, checking social media, and responding to Lyric's texts.

Well, pretended to, anyway.

Without warning, something hard was pressed between my shoulder blades. "Well, hi there, bitch," an angry voice growled. "I never thought I'd get to you."

I squeezed my eyes shut. "Graham."

Holy crap, Jaxon had been right. Not that I doubted him, but I didn't think any of this would be happening this quickly.

"Very good," he said in a sing-song voice. "Butchy always said you were smart. But now, I've got you and you're going to pay for killing him. He promised me I'd get to finish you."

"Jaxon is going to be here in seconds," I warned.

"Yeah, but not faster than a bullet. Get up."

I stood slowly. I still had the back of the bench between us and I really, really hoped Jaxon was close.

"Duck, Harmony!" Jaxon bellowed and I dropped to the ground just as a heavy body covered me, and Graham let out a squeal, then a grunt.

"I can't breathe," I rasped and the body shifted.

"Sorry," he said, and I recognized Cheese's voice.

"Get off me!" Graham screamed.

"Stop resisting!" Jaxon demanded.

I lifted my head to see Brock fighting to get one of Graham's hands secured while Jaxon had a knee in the middle of his back and one of his wrists handcuffed. Dallas kicked Graham's gun away and then helped Jaxon and Brock get him under control.

"Got 'im," Brock said, and Jaxon removed his knee from Graham's back.

"We're gonna help you up, asshole," Jaxon said, and he and Brock helped Graham to his feet. Jaxon then handed him off to Brock and Dallas and made his way to me. "You can let her up now."

Cheese slid away from me and Jaxon pulled

me up and into his arms. "You were so good, baby."

"I was, huh?" I whispered, shivering. The adrenalin was wearing off and I now clung to him like a spider monkey baby clings to its mother.

"So, so good."

Brock nodded. "You're a real natural. All that stuff about going out to eat afterwards, that was perfect."

"Yeah, that was all Harmony," Jaxon said.

"It was all so natural," Dallas added. "Like you were really planning all that."

"It was on the fly," Jaxon said. "We weren't sure if Graham was listening, so we just had to keep making shit up."

"Well, I'd go out in the field with you any day," Brock said, and I grinned.

"Thanks."

I started to shake again and Jaxon squeezed me tighter. "I've got you, Rufus."

I squeezed my eyes shut and tried not to completely break down.

"We'll take care of him," Brock said. "You take care of Harmony. We'll meet you back at her place later."

"Okay, brother. Thanks."

"Let's get you home," Jaxon suggested.

"Yes. Please."

Jaxon walked me to his SUV and helped me in. Apparently, Cheese had loaded all of my purchases in the back, so Jaxon took me home and insisted I soak while he put everything away.

I didn't argue.

After my bath, I dressed in yoga pants and a T-shirt and padded out to the kitchen to find Jaxon unloading bags of food. "You grabbed dinner?"

He shook his head. "Cheese grabbed dinner."

"Oh, wow."

He grinned. "Yeah, I'm kind of getting why my brothers are in an MC and make recruits do grunt work."

I chuckled, closing the distance between us and wrapping my arms around him. "Thanks for letting me process in the tub."

He hugged me tight. "You're welcome. You wanna talk about it?"

"Actually, I want to talk to you about something else."

"Yeah?"

I pulled away and grabbed a beer for him out of the fridge, and a wine glass for me from the cabinet. "How hard is it to get into the FBI?"

"Hard, why?"

I bit my lip. "I'd kind of like to try."

He raised an eyebrow and twisted the top off

his beer. "Yeah?"

"Yeah, what Brock said got me thinking."

"What Brock said?"

"Yeah, about how he'd go out in the field with me. And Dallas said I was a natural, and even you said I was really, really good."

"I did say that, didn't I?" His tone was hesitant, so I gave him a bolstering smile.

"You don't think I can do it, do you?"

"No, baby, the problem is I *know* you can."

"Why is that a problem?"

"Oh, I don't know, maybe because the thought of you in any kind of danger gives me hives." He took a swig of beer and I filled my glass with wine.

"So, will you stop me from trying?"

"No way in hell," he said, setting his beer down and pulling me against him. "I will support you, no, I will champion you, in whatever you want to do. I knew you'd be amazing at some kind of law enforcement, considering all of the notes and surveillance you already had on the stalker. You were so close, Harmony. I don't even think you realize how close you were." He lifted my chin and smiled. "You've already got a bachelor's in criminal justice, so you're ninety percent of the way there. Admittedly, I would prefer you do something behind a desk, but

Brock and Dallas are right, you played that part perfectly, and would be an asset to any team you were put on."

I blinked back tears. "I love you."

"I love you, too." He kissed me gently. "You gonna marry me?"

"You haven't asked."

He reached into his pocket, then knelt in front of me and held up the prettiest ring I'd ever seen. "Harmony Rose Morgan, will you marry me?"

I let out a quiet squeak and nodded. "Yes, oh my god, yes."

He slid the ring on my finger and rose to his feet, pulling me into his arms and kissing me long and deep. "Tomorrow."

I giggled. "Give me a week, at least."

"Okay, Rufus, you got a week."

I held my hand up to the light.

"Do you like it? It's a French-set halo, two and half carat diamond. I chose white gold, but I wasn't sure if platinum would be better," he said. "We can return—"

I covered his mouth with my hand. "Don't say another word. It's the most amazing ring I've ever seen. If you try to pry it off my hand, it will have to be off my cold, dead body."

He grinned, kissing my fingers, then kissing

me again. "You like it, then."

"I *love* it. It's perfect. Just like you."

Jaxon kissed me again, then he carried me to my bedroom and fucked his fiancé into total oblivion before curling up on the sofa to eat our reheated dinner and watch a movie.

Harmony

Six months later…

"HARMONY?" JAXON CALLED.
"Back here, baby," I replied as I leaned into our bedroom mirror to figure out why I couldn't get my earring clasped. We had moved in together two months ago and our wedding was set for December so my sisters could be part of it.

Currently, I was getting ready for girls' night with his sisters-in-law, and a couple of the women from the club.

He walked in and I stood on my tiptoes to kiss him quickly. "You're home early. I almost didn't get my lover out before you caught him."

He chuckled giving my butt a smack. "Minx."

I managed to get my earring in and then followed him into the bathroom. "How was your day?"

"Informative," he said and washed his face.

"Did you get the bad guy?"

"We did, actually." He grinned, toweling off then leaning against the counter. "I figured I'd be your designated driver tonight."

I narrowed my eyes. "This is girls' night, Jaxon, which means, no boys allowed."

He grinned. "I'll stay out of your way, baby. Promise. Brock's gonna meet me wherever you ladies go."

"Oooh, so I can drink and drink and drink."

He laughed. "As much as your heart desires, but if you puke in the rig, you're cleaning it up."

"Deal."

"In other news... we're hiring."

I raised an eyebrow. "Oh, yeah?"

He nodded. "And Matt wants to hire you."

I clapped my hands. "Really?"

I was currently in training, having discovered my passion was numbers in the form of forensic accounting. In order to get any kind of decent position within the FBI, however, you had to have work experience, so that had been my focus over the past few weeks.

"Yeah. It'd be entry level—"

"I accept."

"It's shit pay, baby. Do you want to take that kind of step back?"

"I'm not doing this for the money. I have enough in savings to keep me going for more than ten years, you know that." I closed the distance between us and slid my arms around his waist. "Do you not want me to work with you?"

"No, I love the idea. And the fact you're focusing on a desk job makes me very, very happy."

I grinned. "I know. So, why are you hesitant?"

"Because I'm never going to see you."

"You'll see me."

"If you're working a normal forty-hour work week, and I'm working the crazy hours I work, it'll be hard."

"That would be true for any job I get," I reminded him. "But if I'm working in your office, we'll have more chances to steal time together."

"You have a point." He smiled, cupping my face. "Jesus, you're smart."

I laughed. "It's why they want to pay me the small bucks."

"You're still gonna have to go through the interview process and it's not a guarantee…"

"Yep, I get it. It's all good. If I don't get the job, I won't take it personally."

"This is why I love you, you know that right?"

"I thought it was because of my stellar twat."

"Oh, yeah. That too." He grinned, lifting me so I could wrap my legs around his waist. "In fact, I think I need to visit with your stellar twat for a bit."

"I have girls' night."

"I just need ten minutes."

I let out a snort. "When have you ever gone less than thirty?"

He grinned, dropping me gently on the bed.

"I appreciate you being in just your bra and panties, Rufus," he said, leaning over me.

I tugged on his shirt. "If you'd gotten home on time, I'd be in my little blue dress."

"As much as I love that dress, I still think you should be waiting for me like this every time I come home." He kissed his way down my body, sliding my panties off as he went.

"Don't mess up my hair."

He lifted his mouth from my pussy and cocked his head. "Bend over the bench."

"Okay," I said, excitedly.

I slid off the mattress and leaned over the tufted bench at the end of our bed. I was now in just my bra, but Jaxon made quick work of removing that and he gave my butt a gentle smack before burying himself deep from behind.

"Yes," I hissed out.

"You okay?"

"God, yes, harder, baby."

He cupped a breast and rolled my nipple into a tight peak as he slammed into me, faster and faster, and I thought I'd lose my mind.

"Now, Jax!" I begged.

His hand slid between my legs and he fingered my clit and buried himself deeper until my walls contracted around him and he finally let himself go.

Kissing the back of my neck, he slid out of me, and walked to the bathroom, returning with a warm washcloth and settling it between my legs.

I sat on the bench and watched him button his jeans back up. "You didn't even take off your boots."

"You said I had limited time." He grinned, leaning down and kissing me quickly. "I prioritized."

I chuckled. "I like when you prioritize, especially if I get an orgasm out of it."

"I aim to please, Rufus." He handed me my discarded underwear and leaned against my dresser while I redressed. "Are we eating here or out?"

"We were all planning on eating at Blush."

"Jesus, you're going to Blush?"

"Yeah, why?"

"Was that Kim's idea?"

"Actually, yes, it was," I said as I stepped into the closet and pulled out my dress. "Is that a problem?"

"Ah…"

"Please don't say it's a problem," I rushed to say. "That place is impossible to get into and Darien got us the VIP section."

He visibly relaxed. "Okay, good. VIP I can handle."

I raised an eyebrow. "What if we hadn't gotten the VIP section?"

"I would have called Booker or Mack and insisted they clear it out for you," he said. "That place is a meat market."

Well, this was interesting information. Not

the meat market nugget, because I knew that, but the fact he could call Booker or Mack to take care of it. "You have clout to get the VIP section cleared out?"

"Do you know who owns Blush?"

I shrugged. "No, should I?"

"Dogs of Fire."

"No way," I breathed out.

"Booker and Mack run it."

I slipped my dress over my head, then turned my back so Jaxon could zip me up. "How did that never come up in conversation with Darien?"

Jaxon chuckled as he zipped me, kissing the back of my neck. "You can ask her tonight."

I turned and slid my arms up his chest. "I plan to, but I'm not sure I'll remember anything she tells me, you know, on account of the fact I'm going to drink until I have no worries."

"You have worries?"

"It's a figure of speech?"

"Is it?" he pressed, sliding his hand to my cheek.

I sighed. "Sometimes I hate how well you know me."

"No you don't." He ran his thumb along my jaw. "What's up?"

"It's the specialist's exam. I feel like I'm going to fail it miserably."

"Baby, you got this," he argued. "If you want, we can go through mine and I'll grill you. The questions won't be the same, but it'll give you an idea of what to expect."

"Really?" I breathed out in relief. "I have the study guide, but I still feel a bit lost."

He smiled gently and nodded. "I got you."

"Thanks, honey."

"You're welcome." He kissed me quickly. "You ready?"

"I just have to put on my shoes."

"Who are we picking up first? Kim?"

"Yes. Carter's bringing Cassidy, but I was going to give her a ride home."

"Sounds good."

I pulled on my strappy blue sandals that not only matched my dress, but did incredible things for my legs, then I grabbed my purse and followed him out to his SUV.

* * *

After we picked up Kim, whose best friend, Danielle was at her place as well, we headed into downtown Portland. Danielle's husband was Booker, who was the VP of the Dogs of Fire, and he was actually working at Blush, so Dani decided to catch a ride with us. This meant we got to park behind the club in the private parking lot, which gave us easy access in and out.

236

Jaxon walked us in through the back door where Booker and Mack met us and guided us up to the VIP section.

"Oh, wow," I rasped, turning slowly to take in the space. The VIP section was essentially a mezzanine above the dance floor. It was a huge, open space with a bar at one end, comfy sofas around the perimeter and chairs and tables in the middle.

So far, Kim, Dani, Payton, Macey, Bailey, and Darien had arrived. Knight, Booker, Hawk, Dallas, Brock, and Mack's wives, respectively. We were waiting on Cassidy and Sadie who would be here in an hour or so. Apparently, Sadie used to be a nun and I couldn't *wait* to find out how that worked.

"Ladies, Train and Cheese will be acting as your bartenders tonight," Mack said, and I looked at the men standing by the bar and thinking how hot they were. "They're also on hand should you run into trouble, although, I'm confident you won't have any issues. You've got Knight standing at the bottom of the stairs and no one who isn't authorized to be up here will get up here. If you want to go down and dance, feel free to leave whatever you want to up here, it'll be safe. Booker and I'll be in our offices, but if you need us, let Dare or Dani know."

"If I want to grind on my man, you got someone to stand in for him?" Kim asked.

Mack rolled his eyes. "Sure, Kimmie, you wanna 'grind' on Knight, Train'll take over."

"Thanks, Train," Kim said.

Train gave her a salute and a huge grin. Damn the man was cute.

As the women shooed their men away, I kissed Jaxon gently. "I'm going to be in Booker's office if you need me," he said.

"Okay, honey. Thank you."

He smiled. "Try to keep your bar bill under a grand, huh?"

I wrinkled my nose. "Absolutely no promises."

He chuckled and followed the rest of the guys downstairs.

"Do we want to drink or dance?" Kim asked.

"Drink first, then dance," Dani said.

"Shots first, then dance," Payton countered.

"Oh, I'm all over that," I agreed.

We walked over to the bar to find Train already pouring Patrón into shot glasses.

"Ohmigod, I love you," Kim said.

"Yeah, I know, babe," Train deadpanned.

"You say that every time he gives you liquor," Dani pointed out.

"She says it anytime *anyone* gives her liquor," Payton countered.

I chuckled. "Patrón is kind of an obsession for me, so you can add me to your fan club as well."

Train tipped the bottle toward me. "Glad to have you."

"Let's dance!" Kim demanded, so we followed her down the stairs.

We filed onto the dance floor and I couldn't stop a giggle when Kim stopped on the way down to 'grind' on her husband. He grinned, but stood totally still while she danced around him. Lordy, they were pretty people. A lot of the patrons stopped to watch the show which seemed to spur Kim on. After a few minutes, she kissed him, then joined us on the floor.

I'd danced my ass off for about twenty minutes when pain in my ankle had me bowing out and heading back upstairs. I flopped onto a sofa and unstrapped my heels, dropping them on the floor next to me.

Train walked toward me, a shot glass and a bottled water in his hand and handed me both. "Jax wants to know if you're okay."

I smiled, taking the shot and handing the glass back to him. "I'm good. My ankle's just a little sore from the heels."

Train pointed to a darkened window above us. "Tell him."

I smiled, twisting to face it and gave him a thumbs up before giving the ASL sign for 'I love you.'

I sank further into the sofa and greedily drank my water just as Cassidy walked in with a gorgeous brunette behind her. I deduced this was Sadie. She looked like Mila Kunis and was an absolute knockout.

"Hey," Cassidy said, hugging me once I stood. "This is Sadie."

She grinned, hugging me gently. "Hi. I've heard so much about you."

"Same," I admitted.

"You totally want to know how a nun ended up with a biker, huh?"

"Oh my god, yes I do."

Cassidy laughed. "Alcohol first, stories second."

We all agreed it was a good idea, so we started with the alcohol, did some more dancing in the middle, then told stories while drinking more.

* * *

Jaxon

"And then her aunt told her she sucked at being

a nun and she needed to go live her life. Can you believe that?"

"I can't," I said, trying not to laugh.

Harmony was a little past tipsy and cute as hell, trying to relay the story of how Ryder and Sadie got together. However, she was telling me the details backwards and I didn't have the heart to correct her.

"And his sister was kidnapped and hooman *trafficked*," she breathed out, her eyes filling with tears. "They beat her up when she tried to protect the little girl with her."

I knew all of the details surrounding Scottie's injuries from trying to keep the pieces of shit her captors paraded through the doors away from little Molly. Scarlett Carsen was a hero in my opinion, but if you said that to her, she'd sock you in the arm.

"I know they did, baby."

"They are *bathtards*," she slurred.

"I agree."

We'd just pulled into the garage, our trip home quick since Booker and Knight took their women with them.

"Why do people do awful things like that?" she demanded. "Molly was a baby. In fact, so was Scottie."

"I know, honey. I don't know why. It's why

we do what we do, right?"

She bobbed her head up and down. "Yesssss. I want to get the bad guys, Jaxon."

"And you will." I smiled. "Stay put, I'm going to get you out."

I jogged around the SUV and opened her door, grabbing her discarded purse and shoes from the floor. "Ready?"

She licked her lips and smiled. "Are you going to fuck me?"

"Do you want me to?"

"Oh my god, yes."

"Are you gonna remember it in the morning?"

She rolled her eyes. "Remember the conversation we had about wine?"

"Yeah, baby. I'm kind of surprised you do too."

"Well, wine makes me horny, but tequila? Tequila makes me freaky."

"Oh yeah?" I rasped, my pants getting tight. "How freaky?"

She cocked her head. "Honestly? I don't know. I've never been freaky with anyone before, but I want to get freaky with you. It's time to soak my crops, baby."

"Jesus," I hissed, lifting her out of the truck.

"Yes. Exactly. I want to scream that when

you fuck me dirty."

I kissed her quickly before guiding her into the house where I dropped our shit to the floor, lifted her in my arms and carried her to our bed.

As requested, I fucked her dirty.

Harmony

One year later…

"**W**ELCOME TO THE bureau, Agent Quinn," Matt said, shaking my hand.

I forced myself not to squeal like a little girl who'd just been given a pony, but it was almost impossible not to. He handed me my official badge and gun, and then turned me to face the Portland Bureau office I'd be working for on a permanent basis.

I bit back happy tears as I beamed at Jaxon, my husband, my best friend, my partner in every way. He was the man who'd stood beside me and never let me quit. And, believe me, there had been days when I wanted to.

Brock and Dallas let out a holler before they lifted me off my feet and hugged me as they congratulated me and welcomed me to the team.

"Okay, assholes, get your hands off my forensic accountant," Jaxon demanded, pulling me into his arms and kissing me deeply. "I'm so proud of you, Rufus."

It was just the four of us in Matt's office, or Jaxon would have never been so affectionate with me. We worked hard to keep our private life private, and did our best to stay as distant as possible when we were working. Don't get me wrong, we stole kisses in the supply cabinet as often as we could, but we never kissed in front of any of our coworkers…well, other than the three standing with us now.

I smiled up at him, no longer able to keep the tears from slipping down my cheeks. "Thanks, honey."

I had been hired on with the FBI a year ago, after passing every test, exam, psych eval, and even a math test (no joke), but it had been on a probationary period until they felt I was a good fit for the bureau.

After ninety days, I was hired on permanently to work in the forensics department where I made a lot of headway with my career as a whole. What I wasn't expecting was that I'd actually be hired onto the elite Matthew Quinn team.

Only the best of the best were even looked at, and nepotism was highly frowned upon, so since I was his sister-in-law, I was sure I would never have the chance.

What I didn't know was that my supervisor had put me in for a commendation after finding the gnat shit in pepper that solved a really nasty case we'd been working on six months ago, and then my supervisor's supervisor decided to put me in the running for a place on Matt's team.

I almost said no.

Almost.

Jaxon convinced me to reconsider and even though it took a few weeks of thinking it over, I agreed to let my boss's boss submit my transfer paperwork. I needed to make sure that should I get the job, longshot though it was, no one thought it was because of who my husband was. And by the time I actually got the news I was transferred onto the team, even *I* knew it had nothing to do with who I knew.

"Tonight we celebrate," Jaxon decreed.

"With all of us," Brock added. "If you think we can keep Bailey and Macey away from showering praise on their girl, you've got another thing coming."

I smiled. "I can't wait."

"The four of you have the rest of today and the weekend off," Matt said. "Take advantage of it." He turned to me and Jaxon. "I'll see you both on Sunday for dinner."

"You're not coming out with us tonight?" I asked.

"I got somewhere to be," he said evasively, before pulling me in for a hug. "Really proud of you, little sister. You've worked your ass off for this and I seriously hired the best person for the job."

"Thanks."

"Okay, let's go before he changes his mind," Jaxon said, taking my hand and kissing my palm. "I'm taking Agent Quinn home for a few hours. Text us where to meet you."

I blushed. I knew exactly what was going to happen in the next few hours and I couldn't wait to get him naked.

As he walked me down to his SUV, I thought about how rich my life had become. I had two sisters I rarely got to see, but the sadness was soothed by the sisters who'd made me feel like part of their family from the get-go. And when Lyric and Melody made a rare visit to the west coast, those same women welcomed them in and treated them just like they did the rest of their family. I watched Melody in fascination as she let that unconditional love wash over her and chill her the fuck out. She became human again. She became my DiDi again. It was beautiful.

"I'm gonna insist you wear that badge," Jaxon warned as he started the car.

"When?"

"When you're naked."

I laughed. "Oh, so we're getting freaky, then?"

"Hell, yeah we are. I'm gonna fuck you like an Eff Bee Eye agent."

"Okay, Johnny Utah. Take it down a notch."

"Do I need to pick up tequila on the way home?"

"Oh, no, baby, I'm ready for freaky. You just better be able to keep up with me. You know I did better than you did on your specialist's exams."

He chuckled. "Yeah you did. And the marksman's drills."

"Oh, yeah, I forgot about that one."

"No you didn't."

I bit my lip. "No I didn't, you're right. I just didn't want to gloat."

"Well go ahead and gloat...while your mouth is wrapped around my dick."

"Okay." I shivered. "Hurry, honey, I need you to make that happen, pronto."

Jaxon grinned and disobeyed a few speed laws to make that happen.

As I stripped down to nothing but my new, shiny badge, I sent up a little prayer of thanks to the universe. I'd found my happy and I planned to keep it for eternity.